What Readers Say about a
Cascade Award Finalist:

■ ■ ■

"For me, this was a cover-to-cover read! Excellent story of love, learning, and growing up." K. T., Utah

"I loved this book and found it took me back to my high school years as a Gentile in Deseret. What a beautiful example of the real life culture I took part in growing up here in Utah . . . (written) in a non-attacking and graceful way. I am hooked on this series . . . S. M., Utah

"Just finished it . . . loved it and can't wait to read the 2nd!!" F. H., California

"Excellent book. I didn't want to put it down until I had read it all. I can't wait for her next book." K. P., Wyoming

"This is a very well-written, easy to read and actually quite informative Christian love story. Rosanne Croft answered questions about the Mormon and Evangelical religions in this well laid out story (set in Utah) that I didn't even know I had . . . I liked it!" C. B., Florida

"Captures youthful romance, healthy conflict, and biblical truth, engaging us to discover the saving grace of having a personal, intimate relationship with Jesus." ~J. H.G., Utah

"What a great book. It is true that it is a Christian love story, but it also stands on its own as a really interesting, easy-to-read piece of young adult fiction . . .(it) does not come across as a book that is disrespectful to the LDS faith . . . Overall excellent book." B. R., Massachusetts

Believe in Love Series
Rosanne Croft

■　　■　　■

A Gentile in Deseret
Book One

A Saint in the Eternal City
Book Two

For Time and Eternity
Book Three

A Gentile in Deseret

Rosanne Croft

A Gentile in Deseret, Re-Edited Second Printing
Published in the U. S. by
Blackcroft Publishing
Copyright 2017 by Rosanne Croft. All rights reserved.
ISBN-13: 978-1546454762
ISBN-10: 1546454764

Library of Congress Control Number: 2017909030
CreateSpace Independent Publishing Platform
North Charleston, SC

Cover design 2017 by Lynnette Bonner.
Formatting by Polgarus Studio.
Author photo by Ray Croft.
All Scripture quotations are taken from The Holy Bible, New International Version, (NIV)
Copyright 1973, 1978, 1984 by Biblica, Inc. All rights reserved worldwide.

Printed in the U. S. A.

Dedication

■ ■ ■

To my husband and best friend, Ray
and to Jesus Christ,
who brought me out of darkness.

Disclaimer

I gleaned the ideas in this book from personal observation, stories of friends, books, and years of research into LDS teachings. Names were randomly chosen, and any resemblance to living persons is purely coincidental.

In Chapter 2, the quote attributed to Brigham Young that "young men past the age of 21 who are not married are a menace to society" is currently unverifiable. However, the quote continues to take its place in varied LDS teachings to the present day.

Chapter One

Utah Girls

Alex Campanaro leaned hard on his jammed locker door and shut it with a screech. Senior year with a loser locker was just his luck. He kicked it for the embarrassment it caused in a new high school in a new state. Heads turned and eyes lasered through his back. No way did Utah feel like home. Outside the window, he could see the promise of a powder ski season when he gazed at the mountains that girded the valley. He felt betrayed by his mother for moving them here from Oregon. One more class to go. *Then I'm out of here.*

He had to admit most of the girls were drop-dead gorgeous, their hair and makeup perfect as models. A group of boys in starched white shirts and ties passed him, looking like geeks. Who wears white shirts to school? One of them scrutinized him, scowling. Alex wore what he'd worn in Oregon: a Nike T-shirt and faded jeans. Was it his two-day stubble and wild, dark curls of hair that led to their disapproval? Most kids here were preppy and clean-cut, although a few rebelled against the norm with dreadlocks and tattoos. Where would he fit in?

Alex brightened at the thought of going to his favorite class, AP Chemistry. His confidence back, he decided it may be an advantage to have little social life. He could study hard and graduate with honors. A free four-year ride in college would put him on the way to his ultimate goal: medical school.

Preoccupied with his hopes, he cut the corner so fast that he bumped a thick book from the hands of a girl coming down the stairway.

"Sorry," Alex said, picking up the leather-bound book, "here's your Bible back."

"It's not a Bible. It's my Book of Mormon," she answered in a sharp voice. The way she pronounced *Bible* carried some scorn.

"Okay. Sorry." It looked exactly like a Bible, only thicker.

The girl stepped back and stared at him, swooping her blond hair away from her face with one hand. "It's a Quad, and I need it for Seminary," she said.

"Seminary? In public school?" He hadn't seen it in the curriculum.

She rolled her eyes. "It's not a class in the school. It's over in the building across from the parking lot." Her voice was unemotional. "And I'm late."

His mouth went dry when he noticed how blue her eyes were. "Oh, so you got excused from school, huh?" Even as he said it, he thought it sounded stupid but he'd never heard of anything like this.

The girl sighed. "It's an elective. Look, it's always been this way. You picked electives, didn't you?"

"I picked what I had back in Oregon."

"Did the registrar ask you about Seminary?"

He shrugged. "No. Hey . . . uh, I've got to catch my AP Chem class. It's up these stairs." His mouth was so dry he could barely get the words out. He didn't want to leave without knowing her name. Trying to look cool, he blurted, "So . . . what's your . . ."

At that moment, a cluster of girls carrying the same books squeezed past. One of them whispered into the cute girl's ear. As she bent her head, Alex sneaked a closer peek through her long blond hair. Her right ear was creamy pink, and she wore a tiny gold and blue earring. Long eyelashes swept her cheek, resting on it like soft feathers. Even if she'd gone without makeup, she was the prettiest girl he'd ever seen.

"See you around," she said coolly, and then a horde of girls swallowed her and she was gone in a sea of colorful clothing and well-coifed hair.

"*Ciao*," he shouted amidst the roar of girls sashaying down the hall. Then to himself, he murmured, "*Ciao*, Pretty-Mormon-Girl-Without-a-Name." His heart pounded as he took the stairs two at a time and searched for a drinking fountain.

■ ■ ■

In the unfamiliar classroom, the Table of Elements welcomed him like a lost son as he walked into Room 203. At least some things never changed: God and chemistry, he thought, his sense of humor kicking in after an exhausting day. Alex was sure he was late, but there was a seat in front, so he grabbed it.

A dark-haired girl in the desk next to him frowned at the white board.

"Hey," Alex said to her, "what's up?"

Her mouth was in a tight line. "The teacher's late on the first day. You think it's a precursor of things to come?"

"Probably not a good sign." This girl was a kick.

"If he doesn't show up soon, I'm switching classes. If Mr. Anderson isn't serious about teaching, why should I be serious about learning? Just my opinion."

"Here he comes. Hey, my name's Alex Campanaro." Alex desperately wanted one person to know his name before the day ended.

"Madeline Silva," she said in a low tone.

Mr. Anderson apologized and began his lecture. In spite of a stressful day at Davis High, Alex lit up to his favorite class and immediately liked the teacher. He hoped he would be ahead of the others and found out he was, raising his hand for every question. After class, Madeline spoke to him.

"So, have you lived in Utah long?" she asked with an innocent smile.

This was often the first question people asked in Utah to find out where you stood on religion. It was way more than a friendly question. Alex knew it probed whether you had a long-standing family in Utah. It was a question about whether you fit in or not. He'd evaded these questions before, but this time, he answered boldly.

""I've only lived here a couple months. We moved here this summer from Oregon. My mother got a teaching job at Weber State University."

"How do you like it?" she asked.

Another zinger. This was the second fishing question in the "Mormon dance" as Alex liked to call it in his mind. If you answered that you loved it, it meant you were probably a Latter-day Saint, and if you didn't like Utah, well, then . . .

"It's okay. I'm anxious to ski the famous 'best snow on earth'," he said, uncommitted.

They walked together down the stairs.

"Well, what do you know?" Madeline looked amused. "I'd have put you down for a boarder, but you ski! My uncle's the manager up at Wolf Mountain Ski Resort. It's a small mountain compared to like, Alta, but I can get you a cheap ticket. The catch is, you have to take me, since the ticket is two for one." Her hoop earrings shook against her olive skin when she laughed. She looked rather pretty in the sunny light of the high windows.

"Thanks, Madeline." This girl openly flirted, but he didn't mind.

After a nervous laugh, she said, "After school I walk to the Junior High, where my mom picks me and my sister up. Want some exercise?"

"Sure, if I can keep up with you. My brother's over there in Junior High, too, and I have to get him anyway." He wondered how Gabe's first day went.

Once they retrieved books from their lockers, they met at the exit door.

"So do you play a sport? You're so tall, I figure you're a basketball guy. Me, I don't do sports." She chattered all the way across the green grassy field in back of the high school.

"I played high school basketball a long time ago." Alex hesitated. "I had to quit playing when my dad got sick."

"Oh, I'm sorry, your dad's sick?"

"Cancer. He fought it for a long time, but he didn't make it."

"Oh." Madeline slowed down her quick walk. "I'm really sorry, Alex. Is that why you moved?"

"Yeah. My mom had to get a job. Medical bills. It was about two years ago." He remembered the exact time, the exact date, but slid into short sentences to stop any unwanted emotion from spilling out.

Madeline looked right at him, her face concerned. "You must miss him terribly. I don't know what I'd do without my dad. Your poor mom and brother, too."

Alex nodded. He gulped down the lump in his throat that threatened to show up all day. Nothing was the same after Dad's death. He hated moving here from Portland, and he missed his church youth group, but he couldn't think about it, not now.

Madeline picked up her pace again. "We . . . we're getting close. I usually take this side street, and walk up a block."

He was glad she'd changed the subject. "Hope my brother's there, but he might have walked home by himself. So you have the one sister. Are there more kids in your family?"

"We only have two. My dad's a pediatric surgeon, so he's busy all the time. People have lots of babies here! Our neighbors have seven kids."

"We have two kids in my family, too. Me and my brother. Your dad's a doctor? I'd like to be a doctor, too, someday."

"Everyone in AP Chem wants to be a doctor! My dad wants me to, but no, I'm going to be a teacher."

"My mom loves teaching history at Weber State," he told her, putting a bit of pride in his voice.

"Cool. I'd like to meet her sometime. So, Alex, you're not LDS, are you?"

He grinned. "How can you tell?"

"With an Italian name, you're not exactly a WASP, you know: White Anglo-Saxon Protestant. Here in Kaysville, the demographics are pretty apparent. Second, you only have two kids in your family, your mom works full-time, and you're from Portland."

He was relieved that Madeline talked so openly about the peculiarities of Utah life.

She continued, "You have a Starbucks sticker on your notebook. Dead giveaway. I'm not LDS either; we're Catholic. I've lived here so long I can usually tell, and I guessed right about you."

"I'm evangelical Christian, and *si*, I'm Italian. Both sides, but my mom's family actually lives near Rome." It felt good to smile after the tough day.

"Wow. There definitely aren't many evangelicals around here. Are you Baptist?"

"We go to a nondenominational Bible-believing church. Kind of like Baptist."

"Oh, yeah. There are a few Baptists here in Utah." She paused. "I did think there was a chance you could be a Jack Mormon. Your haircut . . . or lack of it."

"Jack Mormon?"

"A Jack Mormon would probably go to Starbucks. I hear they call themselves Cultural Mormons now. It means they're inactive. They don't disapprove of the Church, but they don't believe in all the stuff the regular LDS have to believe in."

"Oh, yeah, Mormons abstain from coffee. I found that out right away."

"By the way, they prefer to be called LDS."

"They don't call themselves Mormons?"

"Not much. They don't drink coffee or tea because Joseph Smith said it was unhealthy. Eventually, his suggestion became a major rule to get into the temple. I saw a Jack Mormon Coffee Shop in downtown Salt Lake. I think a lot of LDS sneak to have some, wouldn't you?"

Alex liked her sense of humor. "I should apply for a job there instead of Starbucks where I work now."

"Most of them can laugh about themselves. That's a good thing. But they don't like us gentiles to laugh at them," she warned.

"You're kidding. Non-Mormons are called gentiles?"

"Look at you, picking up the local lingo." Madeline grinned. "You and I are gentiles in Deseret!"

"Dez . . . er . . . rett? What's that?"

"I'll fill you in on fifth-grade state history, which you missed. *Deseret* is what Brigham Young wanted to call Utah. It's the word for 'honeybee' in the Book of Mormon. You see it everywhere. The newspaper owned by the Church is *Deseret News*. The thrift store is Deseret Industries; DI for short. There's Deseret Bookstores, and well, you get it."

"So that's why there are beehives on the highway signs?"

"Right."

"Whoa. Sounds like I missed a lot of history. So do you live close to here?"

Madeline pointed west. "I live on the other side of Kaysville. We're in Ward 17, I think."

"Ward 17?"

"See, every neighborhood has a local chapel in an area called a ward. They're all numbered. About 350 people go to services every Sunday morning and 350 in the afternoon. Services last three hours! And I thought Mass was long."

"So that's why the streets are dead on Sundays."

"Yeah, it's also why kids are afraid to be friendly to you at school. You would've been going to the Church during the summer, but you didn't, so no one knows you or trusts you. Tight community, huh?"

"All this time I thought I stunk or something."

"Think of being a little kid and sitting through those long meetings. Yuck. I did hear that after the first hour, they have a class for kids called Primary. Wait, here's my mom."

"Hey, see you tomorrow," he said, "and you won't forget to get the two-for-one ticket as soon as it snows?"

She shook her head. "No way will I forget."

Madeline grabbed her sister's hand and got into the car, hoop earrings flying. Even her mom waved to him, every bit as friendly as Madeline. He looked around for Gabe, texted him, but got no answer. So Alex walked back to his truck at the high school, happy for the first time that day. There was at least one person here who understood him. He could forget his messed-up locker until tomorrow.

Chapter Two
The Only Way to Heaven

Jennalee Young twiddled her pencil during Seminary. She hardly heard the opening prayer. Who was the tall hunky guy with mounds of dark curly hair she'd run into near the staircase? Most guys didn't pick up your books even if they knocked them out of your hands. And just who said "*ciao*" in Utah?

How was he so lucky to have that hair? And kind eyes that looked right through her? He spoke gently, with none of the rougher language she heard in the halls from the more rebellious teens. Hadn't he mentioned going to AP Chemistry? He was smart, but not LDS. If he had been, he'd have known a Quad when he saw one, and that it was required for Seminary. Every day she read from one of the four books in it: the Book of Mormon, a King James Bible in the Joseph Smith translation, Doctrines and Covenants, and the Pearl of Great Price. The guy was clueless about all of it.

Jennalee noticed his clothes were grungier than the designer clothes she and her friends wore. She liked understated classics and shopped all summer to get the right collegiate look. This guy wore a T-shirt, and his shoes were old and sloppy. He appeared comfortable, but unprofessional, especially for an AP student. Still, he was extremely good-looking. The fact he wasn't LDS would be a challenge, but she'd find out about him anyway. Her heart beat faster, rising to the knowledge she was in forbidden territory if she pursued this guy.

First, she'd need his name. She could kick herself for leaving just as he was about to introduce himself. But Corinne Jones was taking AP Chem, wasn't she? Jennalee's shy and studious friend from grade school wore no makeup. She'd never even gone out with anyone. Jennalee rarely hung out with her anymore, but she knew Corinne would be able to help her find out who this guy was and why he'd moved to Kaysville.

Her phone buzzed in her pocket. A text from her best friend Nicole appeared on the screen. There were ways to sneak texts during class. One was to hold your phone behind a book. She'd had lots of practice doing this.

I see you dreaming about that dude. NOT LDS!

The text was blunt. Jennalee stared at the words, then smirked at Nicole, who sat across the room. *I know*, she texted back, *Clueless but nice.*

Nicole shot back: *Nice but you play with fire.*

Jennalee mouthed the word "later!" and tucked her phone back into her skirt pocket. She didn't want to get caught texting. With her father serving as Stake president, Jennalee had to toe the line in Seminary. There were more eyes on her than she cared to think about. As a senior looking forward to Brigham Young University next year, she needed recommendations from her Seminary teachers and countless others. And her father knew absolutely everything about everyone.

The instructor, Brother Sorenson, droned on, and Jennalee watched a slow fly circle the center of the room. September air from the open window smelled of wet cottonwood leaves. She reopened her Quad, and landed in the New Testament. Why had she told the guy it wasn't a Bible? To her, it was a Book of Mormon because she rarely read the Bible unless Seminary required it. "*In the beginning was the Word*" was printed on the page in front of her. It went on, "*and the Word was with God, and the Word was God. He was in the beginning with God.*" That's why she never read it; it was incredibly hard to understand.

Brother Sorenson pointed to a framed sepia photograph of Brigham Young on the wall. Jennalee thought the Prophet looked stern, with his long side whiskers and unruly beard. She didn't care if he *was* her great-great-great-great-grandfather, he'd never looked friendly or nice. But she admitted he'd said some wise things.

"The Prophet Brigham Young," began Brother Sorenson, "was absolutely right when he said, and I quote, 'Any young man who is unmarried at the age of 21 is a menace to the community.' Why do you think this is true?"

Nicole raised her hand. "Because if guys aren't married, they cause trouble."

"Trouble is a good word for it," the teacher said. Everyone laughed. "Anyone else have a comment?"

Jennalee decided to give Brother Sorenson more of a discussion. She knew the poor man had failed at many jobs before he'd become a Seminary teacher. He lived on the opposite side of blessedness, and his white shirts had little lint left, making them appear grayish and thin, washed too many times. He saw her hand and called on her.

She took a deep breath. "If a man or woman doesn't marry, he or she won't make it to Celestial Heaven and won't get a principality. Heavenly Father's plan is simple: Only marriage allows one to attain the highest Celestial Heaven."

Brother Sorenson nodded. "Good, Miss Young. Early marriage is best as well, as stated by the Prophet Brigham."

Cory Talmadge joined the discussion. "Are missionaries required to marry within six months of coming home? My uncle did. He was twenty."

Jennalee beamed at him and Cory acknowledged her with a dimpled grin. He was as almost as good-looking as the guy who'd bumped into her, but that guy held an exotic charisma Cory couldn't even compare to.

Brother Sorenson went on in a monotone. "What's recommended is to marry about six months after a Mission. Currently, there is no timetable, but in my opinion, the six-month rule would be a good one to follow. You shouldn't get married too young, but don't ever wait when the opportunity presents itself."

Another hand shot up. "What about women? Are they a menace to society if they don't get married?" asked Brady, a short guy Jennalee knew from Primary.

"Not necessarily a menace. Women need to be in service to the Church, and ready to get married and bear children to be mothers of Zion. Let's turn to D & C Section 132: 15-16 and see what was revealed to the Prophet Joseph Smith," said Brother Sorenson.

Everyone grabbed their books and found the Scripture citation.

"You see here," said their teacher, "that people who don't marry may be exalted, but they can't have an increase, and are *'appointed angels in heaven, which angels are ministering servants, to minister to those who are worthy of a far more, and an exceeding, and an eternal weight of glory'*. Does this answer your question?"

Jennalee didn't have to think much about this Scripture. She had a handle on most teachings of the Church but was disturbed by this particular discussion. It meant that if she didn't marry, she would end up a servant to those who *were* married, both on earth and in the highest Celestial Heaven. It didn't seem fair.

There were more rapid-fire questions asked about marriage, but she decided to keep quiet. Jennalee knew these citations were more than mere quotations from historical figures. They were undisputed as Holy Scripture in her Church. You had to agree with them or you were an unbeliever; to argue was pointless. By this time, most of her friends knew how to sound like they were asking clever questions, but they were really spinning words to make themselves sound good.

Knowing she was attractive enough to get a husband, she pitied girls who weren't, like Corinne. Unease settled in the pit of her stomach. Servants would be needed in heaven. And she could understand why her pioneer ancestors had to be married to survive in a harsh land. Her thoughts took her in a dangerous direction. It was now the twenty-first century, and women still had to get to heaven by marriage? Why would Heavenly Father make marriage the only way to get to heaven?

"Scripture Drills tomorrow!" Brother Sorenson announced. "Class, I see we're out of time, so until I see you next time, CTR! Choose the Right!"

Jennalee automatically glanced at her gold CTR ring as the girls walked out together.

"So how did you like Cemetery today?" asked Nicole.

Jennalee barely laughed at the old joke. "It was less boring than usual, but do you realize we have a ton of pressure on us?"

"What pressure?"

"To get married, that's what. I'll be eighteen in a couple weeks."

"Jenn, it's always been this way. You know the Lord can only work through marriages and families. A person out on their own? They really are a menace like your grandfather said."

"Listen, you and I have never been outside of Utah. At least, not much. We're born and raised LDS. What if . . . well, what if other religions are—"

"I'm not having this conversation. Other religions are not true; they're in apostasy. Only the restored gospel is true. The Prophet Joseph Smith was given revelation directly from Heavenly Father. You of all people should believe, Jennalee!"

"Me, of all people?"

"You're a Young, descended from Brother Brigham himself. Your father's Stake president in Kaysville. People say someday he'll be an Apostle."

Picturing her dad at the highest level of priesthood in the Church shook her a bit. She knew she'd been close to voicing unbelief. "Of course I believe the gospel, Nicole. I wonder about some things, that's all."

"I'm concerned about you. You're like my own sister; we've been through a lot together." Nicole gave her a quick side hug.

Jennalee swallowed. "We sure have. Remember Young Women's camp last summer at Bear Lake? It did nothing but rain. Being wet for a week bonded us. I'm okay, Nicole. I've got my feelings under control."

"Any woman who says her feelings are under control is lying." They laughed, then split, and walked in separate directions. Nicole could never know how deep Jennalee's doubts and fears went. She couldn't tell a soul.

Sometimes Jennalee didn't want to be a Young. She just wanted to be an ordinary girl, who lived somewhere else, and she definitely didn't want to get married until she was deeply in love with a handsome prince who swept her off her feet.

So what was wrong with her? Other girls would've fallen all over themselves to date Bridger Townsend like she had two summers ago. Why didn't she want him?

Chapter Three

For Time and Eternity

"His name is Alex," said Corinne, smacking her gum.

Jennalee had called Corinne's landline. The girl's family had nine kids and couldn't pay for a phone for every kid.

Taking a deep breath, Jennalee asked, "So what's his last name? Do you know anything else about him? He's a senior, right?" Jennalee shot rapid questions in her excitement.

"That's a senior class, Jenn. I think the teacher read the attendance roll as 'Campanaro', Alex Campanaro. Why do you want to know anyway?" Corinne asked, as Jennalee hung on every word.

"I want to know because . . . one of my friends likes him," she lied. Jennalee and Corinne weren't true friends. She respected the other girl, but friends? Not really. Corinne was top-of-the-class smart, but her mousy-brown hair was never styled and her clothes were her sisters' hand-me-downs.

"Alex is way ahead of us in AP Chemistry. He answers every question and asks really good ones. He moved here from Oregon."

"Anything else?" Jennalee tried her best to sound vaguely uninterested after her barrage of questions.

"I noticed he talked to Madeline Silva after class. You know her?" Corinne chewed her gum louder into the phone.

"Dark hair, right? Oh, I know; her father is Dr. Silva. He did my brother's appendectomy last year."

"That's her. Madeline's really smart, too. I saw him walking with her across the field after school. I'll bet he went to her house."

"Thanks, Corinne, you've helped me out."

"Sure, any time, Jennalee. Do I know this person who likes him? Is she in our ward?" Corinne chimed, sounding happy.

Jennalee pretended not to hear. "Got to go, Corinne." She pressed END for the call. Now she'd owe Corinne for the scoop on Alex and would have to find a way to return the favor.

■　■　■

At dinner, Jennalee's brothers talked about their first day of school like excited chipmunks. After they'd gone outside, her parents asked how her classes went.

"Fine," she said, "but I need to get into AP Chemistry. It'll mean having to switch my Seminary class."

"Who's your instructor?" asked her dad.

"Brother Sorenson. Last year I had Brother Johnson and liked him a lot. I could get into his class again."

"I think that would be wise," her dad said, his tone indicating he knew something about Brother Sorenson he didn't like. Jennalee didn't want to think about it.

"What Scriptures did Sorenson cover today?" her father asked.

"Mostly ones about marriage and what Brother Brigham said about it." Jennalee picked at the last of her potatoes.

Her mom and dad gave each other significant glances, and Mom said, "Jennalee, you know how happy we are that our only daughter will marry in the temple after graduation. After a certain returned missionary is back, of course. We're so glad you can start a family in the Valley where the Youngs have always lived."

Jennalee swallowed, as her dad added, "Tonight, Mother and I chose to discuss the importance of marriage for Family Home Evening. It will go along with what you learned today."

Jennalee was uncomfortably aware that, at almost eighteen, her parents considered her solid marriage material. She tried to keep her facial expression unmoving as her thoughts raced. What if she didn't get married for a while? What if she wanted college and career before children? To travel, to see Italy? She loved all things Italian: the food, the shoes, the fashions. But what was she thinking? She didn't have those choices.

After Family Home Evening prayers were over and her younger brothers ran downstairs to watch their favorite show on TV, she followed her mother to her parents' bedroom.

"I've got something special to show you, Jennalee," her mom said.

"Okay." She guessed it was something sacred.

"It's about time you saw temple clothing and knew the symbolism of each piece. I want to show you so you'll be less nervous on that day."

"Were you nervous, Mom?"

"Yes, but you won't be, honey. The Endowment Ceremony is sacred and, as you know, I can't tell you about it because it's secret."

A temple wedding was a dream since she was in Primary. So why wasn't she thrilled now? In spite of being "one of the pretty ones" as her Grandma Young put it, she became uneasy now that she was of age in the competitive find-a-mate-fast atmosphere of her religion.

"I plan to buy your temple clothes next time I'm downtown, so I wanted to show you mine. You can tell me what styles you like."

Her mother had a white dress spread out on the bed. Jennalee noticed the long sleeves, simple high neckline, and ankle length. Close by was a white veil and a pair of soft white slipper shoes. Next to all the white clothing was a green satin apron with a prominent fig leaf embroidered on it, shining like snakeskin under the domed ceiling light.

Her mother talked about the significance of each piece but Jennalee couldn't hear over the rush of blood to her head. She knew this was supposed to be a "coming of age" conversation with her mother, before the event of her future wedding, but dark clouds hovered over her sight and it was all she could do to keep an unemotional front for her mom.

"After the Endowment Ceremony, you'll be sealed to your husband for time and eternity."

One of the boys called, and her mom left to attend him. Jennalee was relieved. She slumped on the bed. Was she even worthy to go inside the temple? Only if no one knew her doubts. She'd glimpsed this dress on its hanger in her mom's closet before, and now here it was, laid out in front of her, like her future. All her life led to this sacred honor.

She remembered when at fifteen, she'd started going out with Bridger Townsend. He was handsome, a good snow boarder, an accelerated freshman at Brigham Young University, with a brilliant future in his father's business. He was then eighteen and all the parents approved of the match. Bridger was her brother's roommate for a year at BYU before they went on their Missions: Bridger to France, and Brent to Argentina.

Her cousin Moab was the first of their generation to go on a Mission, and he was returning soon. She wondered idly if he would get married as soon as he could. Bridger, too, would be home in a few months, but she didn't like to think about him.

Bridger had been hard to turn down when he bullied her into an engagement. She admitted she'd been attracted to him at first, flattered that an older guy liked her so much. He wrote from France, and at first she wrote back and even sent him a package, but something about the rapid pace of the relationship didn't feel right. She knew he could insist on marrying her when he returned because of her promise and the engagement. Did she love him? Not enough. If she could find someone else . . .

Cory Talmadge had paid attention to her today. Was he boyfriend material? There was no chemistry with him. Another thought struck her. What about Alex Campanaro? Truly a wild card, totally different than anyone she knew. She'd try to get into AP Chem and see what he was like. But first she'd write to Bridger and break off the engagement.

Her mother breezed into the room, singing a song from Primary about getting married in the temple. Jennalee sat stiff on the bed and watched her mother hang up the sacred clothes. Her parents had zeroed in on Bridger Townsend for her eternal husband. She took a deep breath and glanced out the window. What would her brother Brent think? He'd understand, wouldn't he? A harvest moon glowed golden in the autumn sky. She resolved to be free of Bridger, free to date someone else. Even a gentile.

■   ■   ■

After a year in Argentina, what Brent Young loved the most was going to the internet café on Mondays. He was allowed thirty minutes for email each week by the mission president. Sometimes they went to an LDS chapel for use of a computer, but he preferred the café's atmosphere. He and his companion, Ammon Carr, cycled a fast pace there today, and he found he'd received several emails. He scanned the list: his grandparents, his parents, his sister, and his roommate from BYU, Bridger Townsend.

Hey, Elder! Bridger here. Things are good in Paris but rainy. Lots of converts, so I'm way busy. I can't wait to get back in a couple months, especially because of your sister. She's the one for me. I see her in my dreams in a white veil in the temple. I'll be back at BYU waiting for you. Hope you make it in time for the wedding. Go Cougars! Bridger

Brent deleted it. After catching his roommate in several situations during college, he'd changed his mind about setting him up with his sister. Bridger's character wasn't good enough for her. He'd hinted to Jennalee before, but now he'd have to tell her flat out.

He wondered how the big redhead's Mission in France was *really* going. He could imagine that Bridger would manage to have a great time with the girls in Paris, gospel or no gospel. How could he let his sister marry an unfaithful loser for time and eternity? So he wrote to her:

Hi, Jenn, I'm okay but worried about you. Bridger emailed me, and I wanted to warn you he's coming home in about two months with the idea he's going to marry you. His character is not so good, Jenn, and I have proof. You've got to make up your own mind about him, I get that. But please listen to your heart. You don't have to get married to the first guy who asks. You'll have plenty of offers after you get out of college. Happy Birthday next week. One more year to go, then home! Miss you, Brent

■   ■   ■

A day later, when Jennalee opened her email, she was thrilled to see her brother's weekly note. She went queasy when Brent reminded her about Bridger coming home from Paris in two months, right before Christmas, in all of his six-foot-three glory.

She knew Bridger wouldn't let her go easily. It would be hard to turn him down, with even her parents conspiring to seal her future. The only person in her family she could trust was Brent. He would defend her choice to break it off. There'd be time to fall head over heels in love with someone else, and choose her own husband, on her own grounds, in her own way. But right now, time was the one thing she didn't have.

It could be that this Alex guy entered into her life at the right time. She blushed to think she'd spoken so harshly to him that day on the stairs. It was the first time she'd said more than two words to a non-LDS guy. Her world didn't include them at all. A guy like him was so rare in her life that she suddenly wanted out of the stagnant pond to embrace the amazing variety of people outside of it.

Her gamble to get into AP Chem had worked, and she started class the next day. She'd be able to talk to Alex. She doubted she could keep up in the class, as her strengths were not in Science. She'd give it her best shot, though.

Taking a deep breath, she sent a carefully worded email to Bridger. She broke it off, hoping they'd still be friends. The feeling of freedom the moment she pressed *Send* elated her so much she retrieved the packet of M&M's she'd bought at school and popped as many as she could into her mouth. She would not be with Bridger for time and eternity. Then she answered her brother.

Brent, Glad you're okay. I broke up with Bridger by email just now. I'm not like all the other girls he likes. I know he'll find someone else. I can't promise myself to anyone yet. Thanks for caring. I followed my heart and your advice! Love, Jennalee

She knew neither of them could answer for another week. She let herself think that Bridger would find another girlfriend so it would all turn out for the best. Released from the secret engagement, she was free, but for her, freedom didn't mean she could turn around and date a non-Mormon. Brent would be upset if he knew she was even thinking of veering off the path.

Funny, her brother had been quiet about girlfriends lately, and she wondered why. She knew of two girls waiting for him to come back. It wasn't like Brent not to mention his latest thoughts on women. Jennalee had offered her brother personalized advice about his girlfriends since junior high school, so she shot off one more email.

A GENTILE IN DESERET

Okay, so how are you REALLY in Argentina? Tell me the truth: have you made any friends, or better yet, had any baptisms? I know how hard it must be, but if anyone can convert people, you can. I may go on a Mission when I'm 19, and I know you can give me good advice. I can hardly wait to talk to you about it. Do you think you'll ask any of your old girlfriends "the question" when you get back? Taylin Pratt asked about you. She's got a cute new haircut and acts way more mature. I also ran into Emma Jolley at the mall. She bought me a soda and we talked about you, of course. She has a good job and shops for clothes all the time so she looks major hot lately. Brent, I don't know if I told you, but I really, really miss you. Love, J

With a lump in her throat, she sent it. Something was unusual about Brent. His emails were short and he never talked about how he felt or what he was doing. What was he thinking? Was there trouble in Argentina?

Chapter Four
Jennalee and Alex

Finally, Alex saw the Pretty-Mormon-Girl-Without-a-Name again. She breezed into AP Chemistry with a permission slip and looked for a place to sit. He was early, and Madeline wasn't there yet, and the desk next to him was empty. He wished fervently she would sit there.

Their eyes met. "Hey," she said, "anyone sitting here?"

"Not yet," he replied, nervous as a nerd.

She sat down, back straight, flashing a pretty smile at him. "So you're Alex?"

"Yeah, Alex Campanaro," he answered, surprised. "How'd you know my name?"

She didn't even blink. "I heard it around. You're new, and I like to know who's new. Where'd you move from?" Her directness left Alex a little spooked.

"I'm from the Portland, Oregon area."

Madeline came into class. She sat one row back, on Alex's right. He couldn't catch her eye.

The girl continued. "Never been there, but everyone says it's beautiful."

"Yeah, Oregon has both mountains and the ocean. Lots of trees, huge evergreens love rain. There's not much snow, though."

"You like snow? Utah has awesome snow." She edged on flirtatiousness, it seemed to Alex, like she really wanted to talk to him.

"I've heard. Can't wait to hit the slopes this winter."

Mr. Anderson entered the classroom, read her permission slip, and nodded his assent. Class commenced. Alex strove to keep his mind on Chemistry, which proved hard with this attractive girl next to him. His eyes strayed toward her. It would be hard for her to catch up in this class. She might need his help. The thought boosted his confidence, as Alex shot his hand up to answer the teacher's question.

At 3:00 pm, the final bell sounded. The class stood and gathered their books to go home. Alex watched the pretty girl wave to a lonely-looking girl in the back of the room, then said as fast as he could get it out, "Didn't catch your name."

"Jennalee E. Young." She enunciated each syllable.

"Well, Jennalee E., are you related to Steve Young, the quarterback from BYU and the San Francisco 49ers? It was a long time ago, but he was an awesome passer."

She nodded. "We're definitely related. He's 3 greats. I'm 4. You should assume all Youngs are related in the Salt Lake Valley."

Alex couldn't help but stare at her. "You mean you're all related to Brigham Young?"

"Right. Brigham Young's my fourth great-grandfather," she said, "and it goes without saying he had lots of children and they had more and so on."

Alex hesitated. "That's cool you're related to him." He kept a straight face as the word *polygamy* popped into his head. He'd read about the many wives of Brigham Young and knew the practice of polygamy was common during old times in Utah.

Jennalee flipped her blond hair with its deep side part. "Ever been to Lion House Bakery in downtown Salt Lake? It used to be one of Brigham Young's houses."

"Haven't been down there yet. I only moved here two months ago and work most of the time."

"Oh, where at?"

"Starbucks. The one across from Zion's Bank in South Ogden. I work evenings, some weekends."

She paused. There was an awkward interval. Must've surprised her by his job as a barista. He accompanied her out of the classroom, and they headed for their lockers.

Madeline waited just outside the door for Alex. "Hey, Alex." Then, "How are you, Jennalee? Remember me from junior high gym?"

Jennalee gave her a wide smile. "Sure, I remember gym. Who could forget those chin-ups?" Both of the girls laughed.

"I'd have liked to have been there," Alex joked. "Heading to the junior high today, Madeline?"

"Not today. My mom's picking me up to go shopping. See you tomorrow, okay?"

"Don't spend all your money. Or hers, either. See you later."

After Madeline left, Jennalee asked, "So you ski, do any other sports?"

"Soccer, a little basketball. What about you?" It wasn't like talking to Madeline; not as comfortable.

"I'm a basketball cheerleader. I did play soccer as a kid."

It totally fit that she was a cheerleader. She was the type: slim, with long hair.

The conversation lagged.

"Are you taking a language?" she asked.

"No, I took care of the requirement by testing out of Italian. It's really my first language."

"Oh, so you're Italian, and uh . . . Roman Catholic?"

Good fishing, he thought. Hedging, he said, "Not me. I go to a nondenominational evangelical church."

"What religion is that, then?"

"Protestant Christian, I guess you'd say." Alex felt the full force of his minority religious views when he said it. He'd never had this sense of aloneness. How could he tell her how much he missed his vibrant youth group back home?

"I'm Christian, too, but not Protestant. Nor Catholic." Her voice sounded hard, sharp, like the first day they'd met. He wished Madeline had stayed to talk. With Jennalee's defensiveness, he thought he'd change the subject. "My parents lived at Hill Air Force Base when they first got married. It's our Utah connection. My mom's maiden name is Giovanini."

"That's fun to pronounce. Jo-van-nee-nee."

"Since her family lives in Italy, we go there every summer." We used to, he thought, until Dad died and we had to move here.

"I bet your mom is the only Giovanini in Kaysville," said Jennalee.

"There are scads of them around Rome, like Youngs in Utah."

"I've always wanted to go there," she practically whispered, "but my parents aren't interested in Italy. I've never been outside of this area." Some of the sharpness left her voice, and her eyes looked dreamy for a second. Alex saw something in this girl, a loneliness.

"You should see Italy. It's the best life, *la dolce vita*. My brother Gabe's a good artist, so we hit a lot of museums. We hike the hill towns, take in the food, play on the beaches all day, and sometimes at night."

Jennalee sighed. "It sounds wonderful."

Italy was so far away, and Alex didn't realize how much he missed it until he started to describe it for Jennalee. It was like comfort food; memories that made him feel warm and loved. Remembering his grandparents and uncles and cousins, he wished his mom would've moved them there instead of Utah.

Jennalee glanced down as she carried her books. She looked so sad that Alex had to cheer her up. "You'd love Oregon, too. Lots to do there."

"Mom and Dad might let me go to the next Utah versus Oregon State football game. They have season tickets."

"Here we are, almost at my locker," he told her as they approached the section of senior lockers.

She slowed her step, as if to talk more. "It's nice to talk about traveling to Italy or Oregon, but I know I'll be stuck in Utah the rest of my life."

"Why?"

She looked directly at him, with powerful blue eyes, her frustration and longing bright in them. "Because I have to live up to my heritage. My family comes first, and I have to do what they want me to. Utah is my home." She dipped her head. "Don't get me wrong, I do love it here."

Alex nodded. "Sure, I understand. I'm not at home anywhere, so I'm going to take a year off after graduation and travel around Europe. My mom doesn't want me to; she thinks I ought to go to college right away."

"A gap year? Wow, wish I could do that, and go to Italy. A whole year in Italy . . ."

"You'd love it. Even the light's different there; it refracts in the air which mutes it. Art and architecture are everywhere, in colors like sienna and umber, the color of the soil in the vineyards. And gelato! I don't just say this because I'm full-blooded Italian." He grinned. "I'd love it no matter what, but I do have extended family there."

"Alex," she said, as if startled out of some reverie, "remember last week when I ran into you? I was late, and I know I was rude to you. Sorry." Her face had completely softened from the hardness he perceived in her earlier.

"I remember you were in a pack of girls moving in a different direction than I was. I ran into *you*, didn't I? It's okay." He tugged on the door to open his stuck locker and pressed in the bottom with his foot. It still didn't open. "I got the worst locker in the building." He motioned in the direction of a guy loitering at a locker across the hall. "Is yours over there?"

She nodded.

He was happy to know she was closer than he thought. "That guy's always hanging out there, but I never see you."

Turning her back to her own locker, and leaning on his, she said, "Except for Chemistry, our schedules are opposite, aren't they? That guy's just Cory Talmadge from Seminary. I had to change classes, so he probably wants to know why." Jennalee started to pivot back toward her locker. "See you tomorrow, Alex."

He didn't want to let her go, and leaned a little closer. "I know this is a little weird, but would you . . . can you meet me tomorrow at McDonald's on Gentile Street? I go there about seven for breakfast. I could help you catch up in AP Chem, and if you want to learn some Italian, I could teach you."

Jennalee's face was close to his. "Sounds good. Seven o'clock? See you in the morning." She shot him a dazzling smile. "And for the record, you're far from weird." She sauntered across the hall, swinging her hair defiantly as she approached her locker. When she got there, she paid no attention to the scowling guy four feet away.

"Hey, Jennalee," the guy called Cory said, in a growl.

Alex watched as Jennalee said "Hi, Cory." Then he dropped a book on the floor so they wouldn't think he was eavesdropping on them. He could still hear what they were saying.

"Meeting him somewhere, huh?" he heard Cory say.

"None of your business, is it?" was Jennalee's retort.

"You've known me since Primary, and you never go anywhere with *me*," Cory said. "No, instead, you're after a gentile guy."

He sounds upset, even jealous, thought Alex.

"We're just friends, okay?" Jennalee was calm.

"Sure you are. You even changed your Seminary class. I'm watching you, Jennalee Young." Cory huffed as he walked away.

Chapter Five

Choose the Right

"Heck, Jenn," Nicole's shrill voice came over the phone, "why'd you tell him you'd meet him? He probably drinks coffee."

"C'mon, Nicole," said Jennalee. "We're just having breakfast. I won't drink coffee, even if he does. He's a really great guy, and since I seriously need a tutor in AP Chem, I chose the top of the class."

"You're crazy, Jenn. You can have your pick of every LDS boy in the ward, plus a certain missionary who pines away for you, and you prefer a gentile to go out with. I'll bet he's even a Catholic."

Jennalee wanted to ignore this whole conversation, but felt like she had to defend Alex. "He told me he's Christian and goes to a nondenominational church. Alex Campanaro is nicer than any of the boys I know in the ward plus he and I have a lot in common."

"Opposite religions isn't a lot in common."

"Oh, and FYI, I broke it off with Bridger."

"What about your parents?" Nicole asked. "They're not going to be happy that you broke up. He was perfect for you and you know it."

Jennalee frowned at her cell phone. "My parents don't need to know. I was never as serious about him as he was about me. And I'm not bound to anybody now, including Alex. He's a friend, only a friend. He's not LDS, I know, but he has as good a chance as any to be converted, the longer he lives here."

"Hey, I know. Why don't we take him with us to the Fall Festival on Friday night at the ward chapel? He'll meet more LDS people that way," said Nicole, "and you can tell your parents he's just a friend." She laughed. "He could be *my* friend."

"Good idea, Nicole. Fall Festival is perfect to introduce him to the Church. He could even come to a Church dance sometime."

"Don't push it. We need to work on him first."

■　■　■

"What can I get for you?" Alex asked. Lucky for Jennalee, no one she knew was at McDonald's that morning. It was more awkward than she thought to meet Alex there.

"A smoothie would be perfect, anything with berries."

When he came back, Alex sipped a muddy espresso and handed her a blueberry smoothie and a side of scrambled eggs. As they ate, he pointed to foods and objects around the restaurant, introducing her to elementary Italian vocabulary. They talked of his summers in Italy, of his grandmother, and his cousins. Alex described them so joyfully she made a silent goal to travel there. She wished her parents would let her take a gap year. It would be heavenly to be in Italy with Alex, since he knew the language, the local haunts, and non-touristy places to go.

"Well, I'm sure summers in Utah are not as exciting," she said, "but I have great memories here."

"Tell me about it," Alex said.

She detailed for him the sleepovers on summer nights at her grandma's big house in Lehi; the fireworks, tire swings, six giggling girl cousins about her own age, tree-climbing, and swimming with the singing frogs in the pond under the moonlight until their fingers looked like prunes. He was a good listener, and looked so directly at her, at times she felt embarrassed. The guy was handsome. That curly hair, and shadowy beard.

"Wow, Jennalee, you're so lucky to have a big family. In my Italian family, I have only one cousin my age, give or take. Sounds like so much fun, I'm envious."

"I know. I'm grateful to have had such a good childhood. I'm close to my grandma, but my wonderful grandpa died when I was seven. Grandma keeps the farm going, and it's given us a lot of happy times. Were you here in Utah on July 24th?"

"Yeah, we moved into our rental house mid-July. We were in a motel before that."

Jennalee heard the misery in his voice, but chose not to address it. "Then you were here for Pioneer Day, a State holiday. Did you see the parade and fireworks? We always go to the Ogden Rodeo. I'm telling you, it's the best part of summer, Alex. Everyone dresses like pioneers, and my cousins and I usually get to ride on a float in the parade."

He smiled a tight line. "All I remember is I had to drive around the parade. I wondered what it was about. My dog freaked out all night with the fireworks. So is it like a History Day?"

"Pioneer Day commemorates when Brigham Young first entered the Salt Lake Valley with a group of tired pioneers and said, 'This is the place.'"

"Hmm. I had to work, and the parade made me late. See, I have to pay for my cell phone and my truck insurance. I work holidays."

"On Pioneer Day, everything's closed," she said.

"Starbucks wasn't. I noticed everything's closed on Sundays, too. The streets are deserted. Even if they're open, a big store like Walmart isn't crowded."

She could see it was all new to him. "Sundays are set aside as the Sabbath. We're not allowed to buy in the stores or go anywhere besides Church. We have to stay at home with our families. All day."

"My mom said that's how all of America used to be in the 70s." He looked at his phone. "Hey, it's almost time for school. Oh, here's a picture of my mom and Gabe, my brother."

She showed him her family, too. "Families are the most important thing of all to us LDS."

"I can tell. Hey, I have a question." He paused. "Excuse my ignorance, but the name of this street is Gentile Street. Do LDS really call outsiders *gentiles*?"

"I don't hear it much." Shrugging, she shook off her embarrassment. She didn't want him to think Mormons singled out others in such a way, but she knew it was true. "In grade school the teacher told us how Gentile Street was named. It's where non-Mormons lived when the whole valley was LDS. They even built a Protestant church on this street." Probably the only one for a hundred miles, she thought.

As she talked, Jennalee twisted the CTR ring on her finger. Was she faithful to follow what it reminded her to do at this moment?

Alex spotted it. "So what does *CTR* mean?" He pointed to her ring. "I see those everywhere."

Jennalee knew the real meaning packed a heavy religious punch. Holding back a little, she told him, "CTR means 'Choose the Right.' It's a reminder to stay pure, don't do drugs, and stay away from alcohol. You know, do right things."

"I'm impressed, I really am," said Alex. "I believe in doing moral things, too. It's like a purity ring, then."

The statement opened a flower of hope in her mind for the two of them to stand on common ground. Of course she knew the unspoken heavier meaning of the ring was to stay LDS, believe in the Prophet Joseph Smith, and the Book of Mormon. No doubt it also implied a girl should stay away from dark handsome gentile men, she thought wryly.

"Oh, Alex, look at the time. And we never even got to study AP Chem. We'll have to meet here same time tomorrow," she said. She liked him in her heart. She liked his honesty, his earnest, caring face.

"Sure, bring your book next time, it might help. You know Mr. Anderson gives pop quizzes, so we'd better study a lot." He flashed a grin.

They slowly walked to their cars. The humidity of the foggy September morning made his hair even wilder, surrounding his Roman featured face. She took a second to appreciate how perfectly aligned his features were, framed in waves of hair. His eyes were large, and yes, innocent. She wondered if he'd ever had a serious girlfriend. He was pretty smooth when he asked her out, so she thought he had.

"You know what, though?" he asked.

"What?" She didn't expect his deep voice to resonate in her mind like cello

29

music floating through the fog. Alex Campanaro was unlike any of the boys she'd ever known.

"Tomorrow it'd be easier if I picked you up in my truck. I can take you to school." Alex opened her car door. "And you'll save gas."

"Good idea. I'll text my address. We can take turns, though. Saves your gas, too."

"It's a date, then," Alex said as they stood outside facing each other in the mist, "a study date."

She laughed. "A date? Going out to breakfast to study Chemistry together. Works for me!" What a happy thought. He'd expressed exactly what she'd hoped for: seeing him again. Every day.

Later, she remembered the fog, his hair, and his voice all in one bittersweet memory. A forever kind of memory.

■ ■ ■

At their next breakfast, Jennalee summoned the courage to ask him to Fall Festival. He didn't hesitate when he said yes. A step closer for them to *really* go out together. She looked forward to representing her Church to him. Possibly he'd convert.

But, deep down, in an uncomfortable way, she liked him best the way he was.

■ ■ ■

Alex rode with Nicole and Jennalee to their ward's chapel. He saw no banners or signs advertising the Festival like there would be at any other church. The girls led him to the center gymnasium where he recognized some kids from high school with younger brothers and sisters and their parents. A sit-down dinner of spaghetti and meatballs served by the Boy Scouts kicked off the festival. Then tables were cleaned up and moved, and the games began.

Jennalee's entire family was there, even her father, who interacted with the youngest boys in a game of beanbag throw. Children ran around, sugared up from the candy and goodies on the decorated tables.

It was unsophisticated, but Alex thought the party was warm, wholesome, and real. These were, after all, the sons and daughters of genuine pioneers, and old-fashioned games were fitting to pass on to the next generations. The high school crowd stood next to a tub of water as a girl dropped apples into it.

"I've never bobbed for apples, but I'll try." Alex put his hands behind his back voluntarily, knelt on the tarp, and stuck his head into the tub. He could hear Jennalee and Nicole snapping pictures on their phones behind him as he missed every apple and came up wetter each time. The two girls ended up on the floor, laughing at him. Then Nicole disappeared to chase down one of her boisterous brothers.

"Wait a minute. This is hard! You try it," he told Jennalee, whipping his soaked head in a wild circle to get her wet, too.

"My hair! You have no idea how long it took to get it this way," she said, "I'll play any other game but this one."

His soaked hoodie dripped on the tarp. Alex shook his hair like a dog, spraying her again. "Anyone have a towel?"

Nicole showed up with one, but his wet hoodie needed to come off.

"Boston!" Jennalee called to her brother, "get a dry shirt for Alex from the lost and found."

The young teen boy ran out of the gym, returning with a sweatshirt. Alex couldn't help but snicker at the blue and gray lettering. "BYU? Me? I doubt I'll ever go there."

A few heads turned, mouths frowning.

"With your mom a teacher at Weber State, why would you?" Jennalee said loudly over the din. It was as if she had to cover the mistake he'd made. He realized he sounded like he was dissing BYU. *Another blooper for a gentile*, he thought.

"Right. I can't believe I got so wet." He took off his hoodie and began to remove the soaked Hollister T-shirt under it.

In a flash, Boston stepped toward him, saying, "Alex, you better change in the bathroom. See, there's uh, too many women around here."

Jennalee nodded at him, her eyebrows high.

He paused. It seemed like everyone stared. "Yeah, okay." He followed as

Boston led him to the men's room. *Another cultural difference.* Modesty in this case was not only a virtue, but a litmus test.

■　　■　　■

"Too bad," Nicole whispered. "We almost got a six-pack show right here in the chapel."

"He didn't know," Jennalee chided. How could Alex know modesty is required of all Church men and women?

"No, but now everyone else knows he's not LDS," Nicole said. "Or not a worthy member, anyway."

Some ward members murmured and stared, but some just went about their own business. Jennalee wanted people to think Alex was a friend from another ward, but now it was obvious he wasn't a Mormon. He didn't act like one.

"I don't think anyone noticed," Jennalee said, trying to convince herself. "Good thing Boston was here."

Nicole rolled her eyes. "It's our plan, Jenn. We invited a non-LDS guy so he'll be introduced to the one true religion. It's what we're supposed to do. Mom said President Gordon B. Hinckley, rest his soul, said we should be kinder and more inclusive to non-LDS."

Jennalee shook her head from side to side. "I wish my parents would think the same way. I wonder what they'll say."

"They'll know we tried to help him by inviting him."

Jennalee absorbed the stares and whispers that were now evident. Some adults followed the action over by the apple tub with interest. She spotted her dad looking at her from a tight group in a corner of the room. What did he think of Alex? And how important was her dad's opinion? *Very,* she decided.

Her mom was in the kitchen at the time, so she wouldn't know about Alex's blunder. Earlier, Jennalee introduced him to her parents as a friend from high school. Both were gracious and kind to him, which made her happy.

She suddenly thought about how hard it must've been for Alex to move and adjust to a new environment during senior year. She could see how he tried to fit in. Why should she care about the critical stares of these people? They never got to know any non-LDS, being too afraid of the sectarian world. But was the answer to shun non-Mormons? Defiance rose inside and she determined to include Alex in her group at school. She held a vital interest to impress him with her life and religion. A *vital* interest.

Chapter Six
Doubts and Worries

Alex stared at himself in the men's room mirror, dimly lit under fluorescent light. The BYU sweatshirt looked good on him, and he was ready to go out again. Or was he? This was unlike any other church he'd been to. Good people, really awesome people. You could say what you wanted about the LDS Church, he thought, but as far as he could see they had made a good life for themselves.

In all of his church-going life, he'd never seen such calibrated organization, with patient women cooking in practiced harmony and cheerful Boy Scouts serving the meal. It wasn't any old potluck, but a sumptuous spaghetti dinner with home-made marinara and meatballs, garlic bread, and fresh salad. Serving food to 200 people in such an efficient way amazed him.

When he'd met Jennalee's mother, she looked young enough to be her sister, with the same blond hair and blue eyes. Her dad was kind but distant, even while he shook his hand. What father wouldn't be cautious with a gorgeous daughter like Jennalee? He probably wondered what Alex's intentions were.

There was something, though . . . he couldn't capture it. A discomfort unsettled his soul. It must be great to have family and Church support like this, yet their culture was peculiar. He knew the LDS had a different twist on Christianity, but how could they be totally wrong?

He left the bathroom and tried to find his way back to the gym through the dark hallway. He only had to follow muffled noises coming from the central gym, but there were countless doors with numbers on them, and they all looked alike. When he tried the knobs, he found most of them were locked.

Boston was long gone, and Alex was lost. It was as if he'd entered another country and didn't know a word of the language. Why had he come? It was all so foreign to him. The darkened hallway circled around the gym, but he'd forgotten which way he'd come and which door to open to get back inside. The word *labyrinth* came to mind as he continued down the winding hall to the front of the building where they had come in. Relieved at the sight of the familiar, he found no one there. They were all inside the gym.

Alex caught sight of a huge painting on the wall. It was the most unusual picture of Jesus he'd ever seen. Jesus, dressed as he would be in any Protestant Sunday school paper or flannel board, stood among buildings that were not like those of his native land, Israel. They looked like Mayan pyramids. The Native Americans pictured backed off from Jesus with fear on their faces, yet Jesus appeared calm, like he was about to speak. A few ruined rocks lay in the foreground, as if an earthquake had just occurred.

Alex studied the painting. He didn't realize Jennalee and Nicole had found him in the foyer and came up behind him.

"Do you like this painting?" asked Nicole.

He jumped at her voice. "Yes, but I've never seen one like it anywhere."

"It's a scene from the Book of Mormon," Jennalee stated in a flat way, "of Christ in the New World."

Alex's many trips through the museums of Europe kicked in. "It's well painted. Look at the brushwork on the architecture and clothing. Good composition, too, a lot like Raphael's 'School of Athens', but Jesus in this setting is one I'm not familiar with at all."

"The Book of Mormon teaches that Jesus Christ came to the Americas with the gospel," Jennalee said in a quick way, "so it's the artist's portrayal of Jesus with the Nephites."

Alex tried to be agreeable by nodding. "Okay. Hey, I've got to get home. You can explain it to me on the way. I'll give this sweatshirt back after my mom washes it."

"No hurry. It's from the lost and found."

"We could tell you about the Nephites and Lamanites," said Nicole, "but you can read it for yourself in the Book of Mormon."

She dipped inside a glass enclosed office for a moment and came out with a blue book, thinner than the one he'd knocked out of Jennalee's hand that day on the stairwell. "Here," she said, offering the book to him, "is your complimentary copy."

■　■　■

On the way home, Alex sat in the front passenger seat as Jennalee drove. Nicole sat in the back and explained that the LDS believe the native people of the New World were actually the lost tribes of Israel, and Jesus came to them with Good News of the gospel.

Alex listened, unable to comprehend this different story about Jesus. Nothing he'd ever learned in the Bible compared to it. Nicole evidently didn't notice his silent demeanor and kept talking.

"I don't have all the answers," Nicole said. "Our missionaries can explain so much more to you than me and Jenn."

"They study so they can answer any question," Jennalee added.

Alex watched her face in the glow of the street lights. She looked immovable and serene, but something under the surface showed a hint of agitation. Nicole talked nearly the whole way home about the Book of Mormon.

With a shock, he realized Jennalee actually believed Jesus went to Central America. And she wanted him to believe it, too. He was flattered in an odd way because it meant she was interested in a long-term relationship with him. But it sounded like pure fiction to him. He hadn't banked on changing his own biblical faith for a girl, not even this girl. Still, he should give it a chance, have an open mind. Part of it sounded okay. What harm could there be to ask questions and learn more?

Alex knew life in Utah would compel him and his mom and brother to discuss religion with Mormons. It was inevitable. So without quite knowing how, he agreed with the girls that the LDS missionaries could come to his house and talk to him about the questions he had.

Why not? He'd take a casual look into the LDS faith with little investment on his part. Living among the majority religious group of people in Utah was way different than he'd expected. Why not try to belong in some way to this awesome group of people? And he really wanted to go out with this beautiful girl, no matter what religion stood in the way. The only thing was, he'd have to explain the appearance of two well-groomed young men in white shirts and dark suits ringing the bell on his mother's doorstep.

■　　■　　■

After Fall Festival, his relief to get out of the car and back into the familiar safety of his house was palpable. He stared at the poster of the David Crowder Band on his wall. Picking up his Bible, he leafed through it, looking for something unfindable at that moment. The little blue paperback Book of Mormon beckoned him from the bed where he'd thrown it. He opened it. It was set up with chapters and verses like the Bible. The title was: *The Book of Mormon, Another Testament of Jesus Christ.* That alone sounded strange to him, since he'd lived all his life with only the Old and New Testaments of the Bible. No more, no less.

So unfamiliar was he of Mormon titles and names he had to read them aloud: "Nephi, Alma, Moroni, Helaman, and Ether." Alex read a little of the King James English, shook his head and put the book in his sock drawer. The Mormons he'd met were great people, but exactly what did they believe? Is it really so different than the Christianity I've been taught?

He wished his family hadn't moved to Utah. He wanted to go back to the world he knew in Portland. It could get tough being the only born-again Christ-follower in a sea of LDS; he didn't fit in. Were they all out to convert him? But maybe they weren't so wrong after all. Confusion invaded his soul as he left his room.

The sound of the TV flooded the living room. "Want to play a game of chess?" he asked his brother Gabe, who sat on the couch eating a cheese sandwich. His brother looked a little cranky after school; he could tell.

"Sure," Gabe said, "let me go get a bowl of ice cream. You want one?"

Alex nodded. His mother had faculty meeting on Thursday evenings, and dinner would be out of the refrigerator. Good thing he'd eaten that spaghetti, because he and Gabe usually ate ice cream for dinner on Thursdays. "Just a small bowl," he said, "I already ate."

"You were out with that Mormon girl, huh?" Gabe said, handing him a bowl.

"How do you know she's Mormon?"

"Aren't all the blondes here Mormon? I mean a lot of them came from Scandinavia and the British Isles, way back when." Gabe started setting up the pawns on the chess board.

"Yeah, well, I went to a Fall Festival at her Church."

"Any fun?"

"You would've liked it. They had a humongous spaghetti dinner, and even though the games were kind of old-fashioned, yeah, it was fun. I went bobbing for apples."

"That must be why you're wearing a BYU shirt. You got wet?"

Alex took one of his brother's pawns. "That's for not paying attention."

In half an hour Gabe beat him with a checkmate. "I can only beat you when you're tired. This was too easy."

Tired wasn't the word. Alex's focus was lost, his steady reasoning abilities fractured. He knew he had to sort this out somehow, so he texted his friend Tony Morris from his new youth group.

A few minutes later, his friend was at the door. "So you wanted to hang out?" Tony asked, holding a huge bag of potato chips.

They went to Alex's bedroom. "Want some Ranch with those?" asked Alex.

Tony shook his head while crunching some chips.

"So, I literally ran into this gorgeous girl last week," Alex began, telling Tony the whole story, with one omission.

"Let me guess. This girl who has you all twitter pated is a Mormon, because I haven't seen too many gorgeous women at youth group lately."

"Tony, c'mon, there're some really pretty ones there. But Jennalee is . . ."

"Stick to the facts, Alex. Get that warm and fuzzy look off your face and tell me on a scale of 1 to 10 how Mormon she is."

"What do you mean, *how* Mormon?"

"Does her family go to Church all the time or once in a while? Does she go to Seminary?"

"I was just at her Church's Fall Festival, and her family was there. And she definitely goes to Seminary," Alex told him.

Tony gave a long, slow whistle. "I don't think this is a good idea, Alex."

"But she's awesome, really moral with family values. In fact, she'd make a good born-again Christian." He had a nervous twinge in his stomach when he said it.

Tony lifted an eyebrow. "So you say, but let me tell you the facts. I've lived in Utah all my life, and holey moley, you're barking up the wrong tree. LDS don't become born-again easily, and they think they know Jesus better than you do. Did you know they have to give up their families if they ever change religions?"

"You mean their families turn against them?"

"Think about it. Everything about their religion is centered on family. Even in eternity, they'll be sealed to their families, so they stand to lose everything if they're not a practicing member of the Church."

Alex nodded. "I get it. Her parents would be really mad if she didn't want to go to their Church anymore."

Tony shrugged. "It's ten times more than that with them. But yeah, think how mad our parents would be if we became Mormons, right? They might even think we were going to hell."

"Probably, but I know my mom and Gabe would never disown me."

"Most LDS don't disown their kids, either, but it's a huge thing for them to change religions, and she's been taught since she was born that it's the best church." Both his eyebrows were raised now. "What's her name, anyway?"

"Jennalee Young."

Tony whistled again. "Great, Alex, you didn't just run into any LDS girl, but a *Young*! Definitely a 10. She's got a pedigree deeper than any fool like you who falls for her."

"Give me a chance."

"I'm sticking to my guns. You shouldn't go out with her. Don't underestimate the extreme pressure to be a perfect Mormon. Her life's cut out for her, and you're not in it, dude."

Alex knew Tony was right, but he wanted to argue anyway. "I could be in her life; she likes to hear my point of view because I'm not from Utah. She said she wants a different life. In fact, I'm getting to know her pretty well. We study AP Chem together."

"You don't know what you're getting into, Alex. Does her family know you exist?"

"I met them at the Festival. She's got four little brothers and her oldest brother's on a Mission. I think they liked me okay. Hey, what if you meet her? Then you can tell me what you really think. I'm dating her anyway, no matter what you say, but I want you to meet her."

"What about at the football game tomorrow? Ben Lomond plays your school on our turf. I have to be there early in my new band uniform," Tony said, looking disgusted, "so meet me at the concessions stand before the game."

"What's the matter? Don't you like your band uniform?"

"Nope. You'll see why when you get there." Tony threw a pillow at Alex and hit him in the face as potato chips went flying. Then Alex attacked him with more pillows and they ran out to the living room where Gabe was eating a second bowl of ice cream on the couch.

"Go get Titus," Gabe said, "he'll eat up all those chips and you won't even have to clean them up."

Alex called the dog and they returned to his room.

"You're a wild man," said Alex, "making a mess like this."

"Your dog loves chips, doesn't he?"

"Tony, tell me again why a born-again Jesus follower can't date a Mormon?"

"Is that a rhetorical question?" Tony asked, snorting a tiny bit.

"No, I mean it as a real question."

"You know the answer," Tony said, "and it's negative. You shouldn't go there, Alex, and I'm saying this as your friend. We outsiders in Utah can look, but not touch, if you know what I mean. Otherwise, you're going to get burned, big time."

"I could ask Pastor Ron."

"Yeah, you do that," Tony said, "but he'll tell you the same thing."

"I have an idea. I've been to her church so I could invite her to our youth group on Scavenger Hunt Night." Alex felt happier thinking about Jennalee at his own church.

"I doubt she'll go," Tony warned. "Her family's high up in the Church, and she may want to, but can't."

"Tony, isn't plain weird around here how everyone says '*the Church*' like there's only the LDS Church in existence? In the Bible, 'the church' means the Body of Christ, *all* believers who know Jesus. It's not a building, or a temple or a denomination."

"Alex, Alex, Alex," Tony said, adding drama to make his point, "get used to the fact that everything in Utah is run by the majority and the majority group is LDS, so their Church runs everything."

"It can't be true. This is the United States of America. The government of Utah is separated from the LDS Church."

Tony clucked his tongue. "Listen, my dad says everyone here has connections of some kind to the Church. Even if people aren't practicing Mormons, they can't say anything negative and you can't either. They're all networked—businesses, companies, banks, everyone."

"Not everyone, I'm not. I'm a complete outsider."

"Right, the outsiders are the Catholics, the Baptists, and the rest of us born-agains. We're only a small percentage of the population in Utah and outsiders like us can't make waves. Get used to being a minority. We have to know our place with the powers that be. Hey, I got to go. Think about what I said, okay?"

Alex nodded. Far from comforting, Tony had placed him in a bigger quandary than before.

Chapter Seven

The Game

"I'd love to go to the football game, but I have a Young Women's event Saturday afternoon. I think they're trying to change it to morning, so I'll let you know." Jennalee wanted to go with Alex, but this was a new step, showing up at a game with him. For the last two weeks, they'd met every morning to study AP Chem, but usually they talked so much they barely cracked the books open.

"The game starts at two," Alex told her, "and it's at the Ben Lomond field in Ogden. I hope you can go. I could pick you up. I want you to meet a friend of mine."

"If they change my meeting, I'll meet you there," said Jennalee. "I'll probably bring Nicole since her brother plays."

When she and Nicole ended up in the same car early that afternoon driving to Ogden, the silence was uncomfortable. They chit-chatted about Young Women's, and then Nicole changed the subject.

"Did Alex ever say anything about Fall Festival?"

"Only that he had fun, that's all." Jennalee glanced in the back of her Ford Fusion to see if she had a blanket to sit on. She hated the cold bare grandstand seats at this stadium. Sure enough, there was the beloved BYU fleece her grandmother had given her.

"How did your parents like him?"

"They didn't say. And before I could talk to them, one of my brothers needed emergency stitches in his thumb. I think they forgot about Alex. Besides, he's just a friend, remember?"

"You're letting them think that. Your dad will have something to say, especially after he finds out you're going with him."

Jennalee drove through a yellow light fast. "He really is just a friend, Nicole."

"Sure he is," Nicole countered, "a friend you've met every day before school. Are you sure your parents don't know?"

"Who's going to tell them?"

"Don't look at me, I won't. But before your dad hears it through the grapevine, you'd better tell him. You and I both know how powerful that grapevine is."

"You're right," said Jennalee. "I'll convince him Alex would make the best Latter-day Saint ever. He's already halfway there with his morals. Such a gentleman."

"At least I gave him a Book of Mormon. Maybe he's reading it."

"He's the type who has to think about things first. An intellectual. It may take him a long time, so I don't think anyone should push him," Jennalee said, peeved at her friend.

Nicole frowned. "So I'm pushy? I thought it would make it easier for you to go out with him, that's all."

"Alex avoids the whole subject of Mormonism since you gave him the Book of Mormon. It was the first time he'd ever been inside an LDS Church, and I don't think he was very comfortable. I don't know why."

Nicole snorted. "Well, he's still seeing you and even called you to go with him to the game today. It didn't scare him that much."

"It's a lot more complicated," Jennalee said. "He's nice, has good values, and I can accept he has his own faith. Maybe he's righteous the way he is."

"Here you go again." Nicole tossed words back at her. "You know you'd better not go out with him until he hears the gospel and accepts it."

"Don't be so quick to judge," Jennalee shot back. "Alex is new to all of this, so put yourself in his shoes."

Nicole pursed her lips. "If he doesn't accept the true gospel, then you two weren't meant to be. You'll have to own up to the fact you can't be together, least of all have a long-term relationship."

"All I want to do is give him a chance, Nicole. He hasn't even talked to the missionaries yet. He's got tons of homework and a job, so he probably hasn't had time to read the Book of Mormon. Quit pushing, that's all I ask," Jennalee said, her voice shaking.

They rode in silence again. In the rearview mirror, she saw the worry on her own face. She had no real answer for her friend, because she knew what Nicole said was true, or at least she used to think it was true. How much would she have to change for this relationship to continue?

A mere two weeks ago she realized she'd never even talked to a gentile enough to see life from their point of view. Then her LDS world was shaken up by the accidental entrance of this handsome guy into it.

Her heart told her she liked Alex enough to dare to change her perspective. She wanted a new horizon, and dating a gentile could be the first step. Her goals were not marriage first, but last—after she'd traveled, gone to college, and met people from all walks of life. People different than herself. Unless love entered the scene.

"Here we are, Nicole." She parked the car in the stadium lot. The noise of a band practicing brought back the memories of other football games. It was senior year, and she was going with a guy she cared about for the first time ever. He was a friend, but she hoped for so much more. Nothing Nicole said could change what she felt about Alex. There'd been lots of dates in her life; the whole summer with Bridger, for instance, but she never realized how strong her feelings for a guy could be. She texted her location to Alex.

Nicole said drily, "See you later. I'll stay out of the way so you can be alone with your boyfriend."

"You can sit with us, too," Jennalee said, hoping to placate her, but at the same time, hoping Nicole *wouldn't* sit with them.

"I think you should be alone. I might get pushy, remember?" Nicole said, scowling.

"I didn't mean it that way. I'm sorry," Jennalee said, knowing she *did* mean it. She absolutely could not risk the loss of Alex's affection because of her pushy friend. She didn't want him to think she was as prejudiced as Nicole.

"Anyway, I see a friend of mine already in the stands. I'll sit with her." Nicole stared at Jennalee. "You're mixed up, Jenn. As I told you before, you're playing with fire and you're going to get burned." Jennalee ignored her, focusing on her phone for an answer from Alex. When she looked up, the girl was gone.

How could Nicole know that Alex was the first guy who genuinely cared about her? He cared about her real self—not only her looks or her body or her last name. She wanted to get to know him further because he made her feel different, valuable and worthy in a way that had nothing to do with religion, but everything to do with her hopes and dreams.

Her phone buzzed in her hand.

@ Concession Stand! ALEX

Jennalee was happy to hurry, just to be near him, even though her heart felt like it would never stop skipping beats.

■　■　■

He walked fast towards her, peering at the blanket over her arm. "I'll carry it for you," he said, taking it. "Hey, you look great." He gazed at her with approval, almost admiration.

"Alex! Over here!" shouted his friend, Tony Morris. "Want a hot dog? They're two for a dollar." Tony stood red-kneed in a blue plaid Scottish kilt, balancing a paper plate with mustard-covered hot dogs on it.

Jennalee stifled a laugh because she didn't want to sound cruel. "So this is your friend."

She was glad when Alex laughed out loud. "Hey, looking good in your skirt, Tony. Nice legs but a little hairy." He gave a low wolf whistle.

"Yeah, I know," Tony said, striking a pose. "It's a kilt, so don't laugh because we're the Ben Lomond Scots and we're going to beat the pants off of you Davis Dartmen."

Alex chuckled. "That's what you think. And no way do I want one of those." He pointed to the messy plate of hot dogs and introduced Jennalee.

"What about you, Jennalee?" Crumbs of bread fell on the lapel of Tony's navy blazer as he took a big bite.

She shook her head.

"No? Well, then, this is dinner." Tony indicated to the concessions clerk that he wanted another order.

"I've never met anyone from Ogden," she told him, "just you, Tony. So is everyone . . ."

"What she wants to know is, are all of you crazy?" Alex said.

"Yeah, well, you know Ogden's reputation is sort of wild, and history supports that. I'm not surprised a person like yourself doesn't frequent this side of the valley." He looked at her appreciatively, and Jennalee spotted a nod of approval towards Alex. She was pleased Tony liked her.

"I think your kilt looks good on you," said Jennalee. "What instrument do you play?"

"I'm in the brass. Trombone. Hey, speaking of that, I got to go." He stuffed the half-eaten fourth hot dog into his mouth. "Nice meeting you." Tony garbled the words before racing toward the band's roped-off section.

They walked close together, across the edge of the field. The teams came out to the sounds of cheering as the Ben Lomond Band struck up the National Anthem.

"How can he do that?" said Alex.

"What?" Jennalee asked.

"Stuff four hot dogs of uncertain origin down his throat, then play the trombone."

She laughed. "He's funny. I like your friend Tony, and he really is the only person I know from Ogden." Their shoulders bumped as they walked.

"He's my only friend here, so far, and you, of course."

What about Madeline? She wondered if he was still walking with her after school to the junior high to get their siblings. Maybe she could ask him later.

Alex cleared his throat. "Hey, we're having a Pizza Night and a scavenger hunt next weekend at youth group. It's always a blast, they tell me. We call it Pizza Hunt. Think you can come?"

Her lips tight, she tried to smile. "I'm not sure, Alex."

"I came to your Church's Fall event. Now I'd like you to come to mine."

"Yes, well, we LDS don't usually visit other churches, Alex."

She watched his smile dissipate into the crisp autumn air. "You don't have to act like you're with me, if you don't want to. But I'd like to drive you in my truck for the Scavenger Hunt part, with a group of other kids, of course."

"It sounds like a lot of fun, really, Alex. I wish I could, but my parents wouldn't like it."

The bleachers rose up before them. Jennalee sensed people glancing at them. She was riveted to Alex's tanned face and earnest eyes where she could read disappointment.

"Okay, thought I'd ask." His tone was low and he looked a little lost.

"I'll let you know for sure on Monday." She hated to let him down, but knew the answer wouldn't change.

Alex sat close to her within a group of her friends. She folded the giant BYU blanket on the seat and over their laps. He reached for her hand where no one could see beneath the blanket. His grip was large and warm, and her hand fit right into it; cozy as two bugs in a rug, as her grandma would've said.

The remainder of the game was a blur. She saw Tony with his trombone on the field at half-time but only thought about the warmth of Alex next to her, the cold crisp air, and the hot chocolate they shared. How could she possibly go to his church? She was curious about it but knew how hard it would be to get away without her parents knowing.

"I was thinking about you today," Alex began, "well, about us, so I wanted to ask you something. Would you go out with me?"

"Like, go steady? Sure, I will." Jennalee looked directly into his face, her heart pounding. To be holding hands while her friends guessed what was going on between them was fun, but more serious was what she had just said yes to.

Alex grinned in his cute, lopsided way. "Wow, so now we're a couple, and whatever comes at us, we face together."

"Right, we're official." She could barely keep herself from screaming with excitement. Her friends would have something to say about this, but why should she care?

"Okay, since it's official, you need to meet my mom. I'll take you up to her classroom at Weber State Monday if you want to, after school."

Jennalee's heart pounded. "I'd love to meet your mom." She tried to sound confident, but fear entered her mind. What if his mother disapproved of her? It seemed that Alex wanted full transparency with his mother, while she would have to bide her time hiding him from her own parents for quite a while. A long while.

Chapter Eight

The Real Argentina

"Not enough baptisms! You're deficient!" said Brent's mission president at the meeting near the temple in Buenos Aires. Brent's head was low under the onslaught of words and all he could see was the president's cordovan alligator wing-tips with tassels. Those shoes later appeared in his nightmares.

He looked at his own scuffed shoes and shifted his feet. Months in the endless slums surrounding the city taught him to clean them every day. Otherwise the stench of the open sewers followed him. Today he and Ammon found themselves in the Missionary Training Center, where they were required to report to the president.

"I'm sorry, sir," he said. "The *villa miserias* aren't an easy place to find ready converts. As you know, it's a dangerous place, and the poverty and drug problems there are rampant."

The man in the tailored suit and diamond tie pin remained solemn. "Elder Young, I've heard good things about you and Elder Carr. You reported a needy orphanage you're helping at. While you do that good work, which I commend you for, you must offer every person you meet the restored gospel. Otherwise your help is to no avail. Tell me about it. Who runs it? The state?"

"The director is very open to hearing the gospel," Brent hedged, knowing it was called the Faith in Jesus Orphanage, and the president would disapprove of them working so closely with the sectarian world. He hadn't lied, though. Maria, the director, *had* listened to them at length talk about their LDS faith. "We help carry water every week to the water barrels on the roof. Their water drums rusted out, and we replaced them. We even made one that absorbs sunlight so it's warm, and attached it to a hose like my grandpa did for his milk barn in Lehi."

"Not only that, sir, we work with the street boys," Ammon blurted out. "We're trying to get to know them and their families, but it takes time and some of them live with dangerous people."

The president nodded. "These Argentinean people are extremely superstitious. They cling to their abominable religion and don't trust us."

Brent didn't like his tone. "On the contrary, sir, a lot of them don't attend church at all. I don't see them as religious. Superstitious, yes, but they suspect religion of ulterior motives. They tell us we have nothing to offer them."

"It's your duty to make some headway in spite of it. Elder Young, Elder Carr, I know you'll think of something. May I remind you of the goals set for this year? We must achieve them, so make sure you come back next month with some bigger numbers. Need I remind you, Elder Young, of your illustrious Utah heritage?"

The allusion to Brigham Young never failed to make Brent's skin crawl with pent-up anger, but he said, "Yes, sir. We'll do our best, sir."

Ammon assented, and they headed to the elevator together.

"What are we going to do about baptisms, Brent?" asked Ammon as soon as they were on the street. It was Brent's idea they didn't need to call one another "Elder" although Ammon only agreed a few months before. It was against the rules in the Missionary Handbook, and both of them felt so guilty most of the time they didn't call each other anything.

"No worries, let's go get *asado*. I'm dying for grilled meat. We eat too much pasta." Once on their bikes, Brent led the way to a small restaurant, where the young men endured surprised looks at their white shirts and ties as they sat down and ordered.

"You're a good friend, so I might as well tell you what I think." Brent sipped his lukewarm water. Ice was sometimes hard to come by in Argentina.

Ammon sat straight and tense. "Okay."

Brent grinned. "I'm going to learn how to tango."

"What?" It gave Brent a lot of pleasure to hear the serious Ammon laugh out loud. "Here you go again. I thought you were upset after the meeting, and now you're joking."

"Don't you want to learn the tango with me?" Brent loved playing with Ammon's uptight mind.

"With you? No. Isn't it pretty close dancing? To a girl, I mean? It's kind of racy, isn't it?"

Poor guy, thought Brent. Ammon lived by the rules, because he was afraid to live life. In contrast, Brent determined to enjoy life beyond rules, Mission or not. "Actually, you asked me what we're going to do to get those baptisms. Our president told me point blank that a Young like me had to achieve success. You know, Ammon, all my life I've had thumb screws grinding on me, forcing me to perform signs and wonders. I can't drag cynical people to the baptistery, can I? And I can't in good conscience baptize innocent people before they even know what it's really all about."

Poor Ammon's face fell from laughing to a pale frown. "I know how you feel, Brent." He paused, then added, "I mean about having to live up to your name all the time." He looked around as if Heavenly Father would strike him for mentioning Brent's name in a public place.

"I had to show how perfect I was at school, at church, wherever," Brent said. "Now I meet these people in the *villa miserias*; the little boys playing soccer in the streets, the women carrying babies, the old men without teeth sitting outside their doors, smoking and drinking tea. Do I have answers for them? How would they be able to live knowing they can never measure up to Church standards? Maybe they're better off the way they are."

Ammon stared at Brent like a train struck him. The waiter set hot plates of *asado* in front of them and went away shrugging because neither of his customers seemed to notice the sizzling smell of the smoked grilled meat. Brent was sorry he'd dropped such a bombshell in his friend's lap, but now his true feelings were out, hovering in the air between them. The year of striving for converts had worn him thin.

Brent went on. "What's wrong with just helping them in their poverty? It looks to me like they're doing fine in their chosen faith, if they have one.

There shouldn't be a quota on how many baptisms we get. This should not be a numbers game. It should be up to Jesus."

Ammon's mouth formed a grim, crooked line. "You mean Heavenly Father. And you shouldn't say that about quotas. Our mission president is right about their religion. Their church is the cause of the Great Apostasy the Prophet Joseph Smith wrote about."

"That's what we've been told, Ammon. I'm just saying maybe we don't have all the answers for these people. Even the wealthy Argentineans in the last district shut their doors on us. We only baptized twelve, and I doubt they're active even now."

Ammon grimaced. "The LDS Church is the one with the Lord's sole approval and, as you know, when the Prophet Joseph prayed to Heavenly Father to show him which Church to join, the Personages who appeared to him revealed all creeds held by other churches were an abomination. You know our job is to give the restored gospel to Argentina."

Brent grinned at his earnest and good companion, almost a foot shorter than himself. As timid as Ammon was, Brent came to appreciate the inner strength of the young man who truly was his best friend. Suffering together brought a closeness you never forgot. Ammon carried a 55-gallon drum by himself, using only a ladder and rope, up three stories. He didn't do it for the mission president, or even for the Church. Ammon did it out of love for Heavenly Father and the poor. Brent was like a wretched apostate next to him.

Without complaint, Ammon walked with him through the *villa miserias* of Buenos Aires. When one of the soccer boys broke his arm, Ammon set it, using his Eagle Scout training. Brent was an Eagle Scout, too, but way better at shooting or canoeing than medical skills. For over a year, they'd read the prescribed Scriptures together, ate together, swatted the incessant mosquitoes from each other, and talked about their future hopes. They were closer than brothers and asked not to be separated and put with other companions. Why should he burst poor Ammon's bubble with his doubts?

"Sorry, I really am, I'm just tired," Brent said, sighing. "I'm tired of all the answers religion pretends to have. I know you won't report me, but I think there's something beyond religion. I'm not sure what it is yet, but I'm going to find it."

His friend nodded in compassion, and they ate the meat with gusto, even ordering cake and *mandarinos* for dessert. Argentina wasn't a bad place, he decided, on a full stomach. They got back on their bikes and rode to the train tracks splitting the *villa miserias* from the high rises of uptown Buenos Aires.

Among the maze of tracks and bumpy concrete, Brent spotted an old broom and parked his bike. Ammon copied him. "Need a rest?" he asked.

"More like a dance," said Brent, swooping up the broom, and humming a few notes. A gaggle of street boys gathered around them, watching the white-shirted *gringos*, and Brent heard squealing laughter as he dipped the broomstick in a mock tango.

Chapter Nine

Alex's Mom

Alex had opened up a new world to her, and Jennalee desperately wanted to explore it. The atmosphere at the Weber State Student Union was a first step. She loved the skylights and modern architecture, incorporating glass across the ceiling. She and Alex stood in front of the curved bakery case in the bustling café, craving the fancy pastries. Alex bought her a Coke when he got his familiar espresso, and they shared a pumpkin scone with maple icing.

"Cool Student Union, huh? My mom really wants to meet you, so I'm glad you could make it. She's in the history department over at the Social Sciences building."

"I might think about going to college here instead of BYU. Course my parents want me at BYU because it's . . ." Jennalee hesitated to finish.

"It's what?"

She knew the real reason to attend BYU was for LDS women to meet LDS husbands, but she said, "BYU's more prestigious, but if I came here, I'd be closer to home, so they'd like that, I guess. I can hardly wait to be on my own!"

"Me, too, except with my dad gone, I need to live at home, at least during the first year of college."

"Weber State's perfect for you then because your mom works here, and you get free tuition, don't you?"

"They give me a cut in tuition, but I'll have to work for other expenses. And

I have to save up for medical school. It's ridiculous how expensive it is. I might have a chance to work in Italy for my uncle starting this summer, though."

"What does your uncle do?"

"He's starting an export business for our family vineyard."

"Vineyard? That means you make wine." Jennalee swallowed hard.

"Right. Our vineyard's been producing for a couple hundred years. But we'd be signing up other vineyards besides ours to export it."

Wine was a business so strange, she'd never given it much thought. She only knew of the commandment against it. "There aren't many wine businesses here in Utah."

"I'll say. Strictest liquor laws ever. Impossible to work here. We'd be interested in an outlet someplace else." Alex casually glanced at the time. "Hey, Mom's class is over. Let's go on over."

A light covering of snow powdered the trees and buildings as they walked past Elizabeth Hall where ducks and geese called from the pond in the center of the campus. His handsome lopsided grin appeared as Jennalee commented on how the snow freshened the air. He reached for her hand, and she responded by taking his. It was getting less awkward with Alex, more natural.

His hand was warm and her own cold fingers melted into his, as her heart beat faster. She was in a strange world, getting to know this guy who wasn't LDS. He didn't look or dress like any of the boys she knew. And he was going to be a wine merchant. That was really different. Somehow, though, knowing Alex underlined her longing for the same freedoms he had.

"So, tell me, what does the *E* stand for?" Alex asked.

"What do you mean?"

"The first time you told me your name, you said 'Jennalee *E*. Young.' Aren't you going to tell me your middle name?"

"It's Eliza, after Eliza Snow. She wrote poetry and hymns a long time ago." Jennalee automatically omitted information in an effort to protect her heritage from an outsider's opinion. Besides, why would it matter to Alex that Eliza Snow was a plural wife of both Brigham Young and Joseph Smith? She managed to avoid the pure awkwardness of this piece of Mormon history by leaving it out.

"Don't you want to know my middle name?" Alex asked.

"Okay, what is it?" She watched, a bit possessive of him, as a couple of college girls swiveled their heads to take a long look at Alex. Too long. Those girls could never guess they were on their way to meet his mother, which might be a step toward a long-term serious relationship.

"It's Dante. You know who he was, right?"

"The poet who wrote Dante's *Inferno*?"

"You got it, Dante Alighieri. Do you realize both of us are named after poets?"

"Seems appropriate, we both love literature." Jennalee switched to a more serious tone. "About the Scavenger Hunt at your church, Alex. I really wish I could go, but I can't."

Alex glanced at her. "It's okay. I think I'm beginning to understand what I'm up against."

■　■　■

Mrs. Campanaro stood erasing the whiteboard when they walked into her classroom. She was so tall she didn't have to reach far to erase the top. Jennalee's first impression of Alex's mother was how she exuded confidence in her winter white pants and jacket with a black silk blouse peeking out. Her long raven hair draped down her shoulders in soft curls. Stylish reading glasses picked up the red piping in her suit collar. She took them off, and her brown eyes bore intensely into Jennalee's, her face softening.

"I'm glad to finally meet you, Jennalee. You can call me Gina. Alex told me you like history."

"Especially the Renaissance, but I like American history, too."

"A woman after my own heart," she said. "I just taught a Revolutionary War class. Come sit down a minute. My next class isn't until four." She faced her son. "Alex, after this, can you go home to be with Gabe?"

"Sure, Mom, but hey, he's almost 14."

"I know, but he's so lonely since we moved. Do it for my sake until he makes some friends."

Jennalee spoke up. "He wouldn't be lonely at my house; I have four younger brothers. My brother Boston is 13, too."

Alex said, "We should get our brothers together. Mom, it's okay if Jennalee comes over and watches TV, right? We study AP Chem together, too."

"Of course, if it's all you plan to do." She winked and Jennalee could see where Alex got his lopsided smile.

Jennalee said, "We really do have a lot of homework, Mrs. Campanaro. I'm glad I got to come to meet you today. This is the first time I've seen the Weber State campus. I'm impressed. I may apply here instead of . . ." She hesitated and looked at Alex.

"Jennalee was set to go to BYU," he told his mom, "but you like it here, don't you?"

She nodded as she spotted Professor Campanaro's gaze resting on her son. A moment of tension followed, when all three of them knew the conversational dance had revealed Jennalee to be LDS. The mere mention of the LDS University in Provo darkened the jovial talk and changed the atmosphere. Was it a calculation on Alex's part to let his mother know her religion? Or was he showing he had nothing to hide?

Gina recovered, but her face was a little tighter, wrinkled with concern. Focusing on Alex, she said, "You kids go home for now and make sure Gabe gets his homework done, okay?" Her voice was sweet, genuine. "It was nice to meet you, Jennalee. Did Alex give me your last name? I didn't hear it, I guess."

"Young, Jennalee Young."

Gina nodded. "I see, so you're a Young. Lots of history there."

"He was her fourth great-grandfather, right, Jenn?" Alex offered more information than she wanted his mother to hear.

"No wonder you want to go to the university named after your grandfather," Alex's mom said, friendly enough, but with an edginess.

Jennalee hedged. "You could look at it that way, but I have options. Weber State is one."

"Thanks for coming," she said. "One more class, and I'll be home." She greeted an early student coming into the room.

"See you, Mom." Alex hugged his mother with slow deliberateness. It was a good sign that he loved his mom.

"Nice to meet you, Mrs. Campanaro."

"Call me Gina, okay?" His mom had Alex's easy-going mannerisms.

In the hall, Jennalee said, "I really like her, Alex. I can see you're close."

"Since Dad died, we take more time to say good-bye, because you never know when you don't have people anymore."

She sighed. "How sad that you lost your dad to cancer. He was so young, too."

"Sometimes I can't believe he's gone, and our lives have totally changed. Mom finished her Ph.D. right as Dad got sick, and she had to get a job at the first place that would hire her, so we came here."

Jennalee reached over to take his hand. "I, for one, am glad you came to Utah. But I'm sorry about why you had to."

■　■　■

"I'm not sure your mom's too happy about me being LDS, Alex." Jennalee swung her hair as they walked into his boxy brick house near Davis High School.

"C'mon, Mom's totally accepting of everyone," Alex said. She couldn't tell if he was bluffing. "Sorry about my house. We're renting, and this was the only place that would take our dog." He sounded ashamed of the simple house.

"Oh, it's fine," she told him, scanning the square living room with a hardwood floor from the 1960s. A red Chow bounded in through the dog door and greeted Jennalee with his bluish tongue.

"His name's Titus," said Alex's brother, Gabe. "We rescued him from the humane society a year after . . . Anyway, he's not a very good watchdog. Too friendly."

"I love dogs," Jennalee replied. "Gabe, do you know a kid named Boston Young at school? Is he in any of your classes?"

"There's a Boston in my algebra class. A real brainiac." Gabe had the same lopsided grin as his mom and big brother.

"That would be my brother! I should bring him over here sometime to shoot hoops. I saw your basketball set-up out there."

"Yeah, that'd be fun."

After Gabe finished his homework, the three of them went outside to shoot baskets.

"Tonight, I'll go get dinner since Mom's teaching late. Want pizza?" Alex asked.

Gabe nodded. "Go to that Take and Bake place. Those are the best."

"Don't you cook?" asked Jennalee, climbing into Alex's truck.

"Sure I cook. You look like you don't believe me, so ask Gabe about my specialties. I make a mean spaghetti. I even make Alfredo from scratch."

"Maybe you should prove it sometime and have me over to taste it."

"You're on."

When they returned to the thinly concreted driveway and drove under the crumbling carport, Jennalee saw that Gina had arrived home. With dismay, she also saw two young men ringing the doorbell on the front porch. They were unmistakably the missionaries: dressed in white shirts, ties, and dark suits with overcoats.

Her heart fluttered to her throat. She hadn't expected them to come while she was here. Oh, she could give her testimony if they got that far, but this put her in an awkward position. She'd agreed that missionaries should visit Alex so long ago, and now she had mixed feelings about it. Alex saw them too, and he directed her to the back door to the kitchen where he switched the oven on for the pizza.

"They're in the living room talking to Mom," he said in a soft tone. "Want to stay here and make salad while I go out there?"

She nodded. "I'll come out later."

Through the arched doorway she saw the young men stand up and shake hands with Alex. They looked relieved to talk to a man instead of a lone widow and a kid. She could see by Gabe's face that he regarded his brother as the man of the house. Everyone looked slightly agitated. In a 180-degree turn, she realized she'd never seen missionaries from this point of view before, standing in a non-LDS house.

"I'm Elder Knight, and this is Elder Larson," said the tall one with dark hair. The one named Larson was a blond-haired, boyish-looking guy with freckles. Knight's ears looked large with his close haircut.

Alex, looking a little annoyed, sat next to his mom on the couch. "We're Bible-believing Christians," said his mother. "So I'd love to talk about Bible Scriptures with you." She emphasized the word *Bible*.

Elder Knight hedged. "We could start with the Bible, I guess." He looked straight at Alex when he answered.

The two missionaries sat down with stiff backs on the edge of a loveseat. Jennalee looked away from the scene and started to wash lettuce. She couldn't hear what was said over the sound of running water, but she knew most of it on the LDS side anyway. The Elders would offer Bible Scriptures in defense of the LDS faith and they knew their stuff. But Alex knew his faith, too. What would he tell them?

"I'm a widow," said Gina Campanaro, "and these are my two wonderful sons. Oh, and that's Jennalee in the kitchen, a friend of Alex's." Jennalee waved at the archway, hiding most of her face behind her hair.

"Won't you come join us?" asked Elder Larson, looking at her with a spark of recognition.

"I'll listen from here, thanks. I'm making salad," Jennalee answered, using a sweet, light tone.

"We're sorry you lost your husband, ma'am," said Elder Knight, the obvious leader of the two. "If you need us to help out in any way, let us know. We can paint, or mow, whatever."

"My sons do all that for me," Gina said. "We were just getting ready to eat pizza. Would you like some?"

"We're invited to dinner at a nearby house but thank you. Since we came at a bad time, we'll come back at your convenience. Can we leave you our phone number? You can call us about a time to come and share with you."

"Yes," said Gina, "because I'd love to talk to you about Jesus, the Word of God." Jennalee watched as they pressed a card into Gina's palm. They appeared pleased, shook hands again, and with a wave to Jennalee, left. How strange this was.

Had Gina just said, 'Jesus, the Word of God'? Unfamiliar terminology confused her. Yet, the discomfort also came from the presence of the LDS young men, and she was thankful they were gone. Alex stepped into the kitchen, and got plates out of the cupboard without a word.

Jennalee knew the Elders. A big welcome dinner had been held for them where they sat at the same table as her father, the Stake president, and her mother. Everyone listened to her father speak, and the priesthood holders gave a blessing for the young guys serving Missions. Surely they recognized her, but they said nothing.

"You're staying for pizza, aren't you, Jennalee? We have plenty," said Gina, who had taken it all in her stride. In fact, her face was serene.

Jennalee felt better, glad that Gina wasn't upset. Alex's mother had been kind to the young men and was even going to talk to them again. She was an educated, strong woman, and Jennalee doubted the missionaries would be able to say much that she couldn't counter. Gina displayed a confident faith in her Christianity.

"Sorry, I'd forgotten that it's Monday, and my family expects me home."

"So it's Family Home Night?" asked Gina. "Such a good idea."

Jennalee nodded and nudged Alex with her elbow, hinting for him to tell his mom about their next excursion together.

"Oh yeah, Mom, we have to ask you something," Alex began.

"Yes, we do," Jennalee said. "Mrs. Campanaro, my cousin Moab is arriving from Brazil on Friday. Can Alex come with me to greet him at the airport?"

Alex's mom appeared preoccupied in thought but said, "Sure. You'll be home in time for dinner, won't you, Alex? We try to keep a regular schedule here, Jennalee, in spite of all our activities."

"We should be back by six thirty. My cousin's flight comes in at five so there'll be traffic."

Gina nodded. "Sounds good. You can come for dinner, too, Jennalee. I have Friday afternoon off, and Gabe wants me to make his favorite Chicken Marsala. The recipe is my mother's."

Jennalee's mouth watered. "Sounds good. If I can get out of the family gathering for my cousin, I'll come, but I can't promise anything."

"Why is your cousin in Brazil?" asked Gabe, his cracking teenage voice coming from the dim living room.

"He went on a Mission for the Church," Jennalee answered, "and now he's returning. Families meet their missionaries in the airport to welcome them back after two whole years."

"Is that what those cups are for? The ones up on the overpass bridges? I saw a sign spelling out *Welcome Home Elder Johnson* done in red plastic cups stuck through the metal holes in the fence." Gabe came into the kitchen, removing his second earbud.

"That's a sign for a returning missionary," Jennalee said, "we call them RMs."

"I saw a sign painted on an old billboard up by North Ogden," said Alex. "Looked like it had been painted over with different names a few times."

"Why do you call them Elders? The guys who came tonight were only teenagers," Gabe said.

Jennalee laughed. "It's a title to show they're at a certain place in the priesthood of the Church. They're allowed to go on Missions when they're 18, so I guess they *are* teenagers."

"Do girls serve on Missions in your Church, Jennalee?" Alex's brother sure was curious.

"Not as long as guys. Girls have to be nineteen and go for a year and a half. We call them Sisters."

During the pause that followed, Jennalee watched the two brothers exchange glances, with questions in their eyes.

"Do students take time out of college to go?" asked Gina. "Because I think I'm running across that at Weber State." She put the pizza in the hot oven.

Jennalee nodded. "The universities in Utah give permission. It's kind of a sabbatical for two years. Then they come back and finish."

"Is your cousin going back to college?" asked Alex.

"Yes, he's at BYU. He was in Provo at language school before he went to Brazil."

"So he knows Portuguese?" asked Gabe.

"Right. My brother Brent was called to Argentina. He speaks Spanish. Castilian Spanish."

"That explains why so many professors and students speak different languages here," Gina stated. "And quite well, I might add."

Jennalee nodded. "Well, I better get home, Alex. Thanks for everything, Mrs. . . . I mean, Gina. See you, Gabe. I'll try to bring Boston over tomorrow, okay?" Jennalee hurried towards the front door with Alex.

"Thanks for making the salad," said Gina, "and boys, I guess we'll have our own family night."

■   ■   ■

That evening, Jennalee lay on her blue quilt-covered bed. Scriptures from Seminary today disturbed her and they went through her head, preventing sleep. The main Scripture was *"and God was once man, and man will be like God."*

Could God be a man? And how could imperfect men become gods? For the first time in her young life, Jennalee had a question in her mind about this teaching from Doctrines and Covenants. Should she ask her teacher? It wouldn't be a good idea, she realized. He was a *man*, for one thing.

A cold feeling rose in her again. It came from the depth of her soul whenever she was forced to confront something she knew she couldn't believe in. A hard lump formed in her throat. She'd never make it to Celestial Heaven with these doubts, but nobody knew about them unless she told, and she never would. The Church could put her on probation or worse for nothing more than saying she didn't believe all of the tenets of the LDS religion. So she kept it inside.

Since the beginning of high school Seminary classes, she'd even begun to question Joseph Smith's vision. Heaven would be out for her, because why would Joseph Smith ever allow her into heaven if she didn't believe in his vision? She *was* rebellious and disobedient, just like her mom sometimes said when she was angry. How could she ever be worthy to have a husband? She wasn't sweet like she should be. Would she ever believe as strongly as her family did? She wanted to; she really did.

She pressed her phone on and was overjoyed to find an email from Brent.

Dear Jennalee: Thanks for writing me so fast. Glad you broke up with Bridger. It's for the best. Elder Carr and I have been through so much. He's from Price and he's agreed to be my new roommate at BYU when we get home, so I'm sure you'll meet him. We see a lot here—messed up people, slums, drug addicts, kids with no food. I can't imagine you doing a Mission, Jenn. It's hard. As for Taylin Pratt, I was never serious and she wasn't either. I like Emma okay, and I'm glad she bought you a soda, but things change. I'm lonely for home, but not for those girls. I met some American girls here, nice girls who work at an orphanage. More later. Love, Brent

American girls? She wondered if her brother mentioned them for a reason. She imagined Brent and Elder Carr sleeping that night in some tiny apartment near the slums. The last time she heard his voice was on Mother's Day when she stuck her ear to the phone in Mom's hand. Now she could hear his voice in her dreams, saying, "Don't go, Jenn. Don't go on a Mission."

Chapter Ten

Meeting the RMs

The polished floor of the airport gleamed near the down escalator where passengers met their families. Women tied balloons to children's strollers and relatives held signs or flowers as they waited for a soldier, a sweetheart, or a returned missionary.

Alex swallowed hard when he saw the size of Jennalee's extended family. He already knew Boston, so now he formally met the 'little boys' as she called them: Jordan, about nine, Cade, eight, and the youngest, Logan, who was seven.

Jennalee introduced Alex to every uncle, aunt, and cousin, making him shake more hands than he could count. It was like he was meeting a whole congregation. Jennalee's Grandma Young drew him aside.

"Young man," she said, "Jennalee is the apple of my eye, so be good to her, hear? I must admit, you two are a good-looking couple."

"Thank you, ma'am."

"Call me Grandma, since I have a notion you'll be one of us soon." She winked a wrinkly eyelid.

Did she mean he'd become one of the family or one of the Mormons? At least he had one ally in the Young family. She reminded him of his own grandmother in Rome and he was sure Nonna, too, would approve of them as a couple. It made him realize how important family approval is when making decisions about dating and marriage.

Her father was outfitted in a dark suit, and her mother in a tailored dress and jacket. Someone handed him an American flag while everyone glanced up to the top of the escalator for their loved one. A literal crowd of Youngs filled the landing below the escalator, and she and Alex stood amongst them, together, but not holding hands. Logan raised a poster with huge letters: WELCOME HOME ELDER YOUNG!

"We can use that sign when Brent gets home in September," Jennalee told Alex. "I miss him terribly."

"He still has ten months, then? That's a long time. Hey, I met your Grandma Young, she's cool."

"She likes you, too, I can tell. Since she's here, I should go home after this. Tell your mom I would've loved to have come to dinner, but we're having a crowd, and I have to help my mother. Grandma will be spending the night since she lives down in Lehi and it's too hard to take her home." He saw her get distracted by another family who entered the atrium and situated themselves to the right of the escalator.

She immediately looked at her father, and Alex followed her eyes with his own. Rulon Young's brows knitted as he stared sternly at Jennalee. Sudden tension rose between those two like smoke from a fire. Mr. Young was taller than Alex, and his expression up to this point had been unreadable, but now it was clearly disapproval.

"There he is!" shouted Jordan, with Logan echoing him. They idolized their cousin; Alex could see that.

"Here, Moab!" Logan waved his poster up and down.

The returning missionary rode the escalator down, waving to the crowd and flashing perfect teeth. Alex saw Jennalee look beyond her cousin to another clean-cut guy behind him on the escalator. His dark reddish hair set him apart from any of the others, and Alex watched as Jennalee's pretty face expressed utter shock.

She glanced around, her panic instantly camouflaged by a plastic smile. Blotches of pink spots grew on her neck as she turned away from the arena to tell Alex, "I'm going to the rest room. Be right back."

Alex shrugged. "Anything wrong?"

"Nothing. I'll be back." She hurried away, leaving him standing alone in a sea of people. Her family had closed in on Moab, with women hugging and kissing him, surrounding him. The other missionary's family did the same, tousling his short-trimmed hair and patting him on the back.

Jennalee knows that guy, he thought. Alex moved back and caught Boston on the outskirts of the crowd. "Who's the red-haired dude just home from a Mission over there?" he asked him.

Boston smirked. "How much will you give me if I tell?" he teased.

"How about I play basketball with you for a week?"

Boston gave in. "Sure. His name is Bridger Townsend. He went out with Jennalee for a whole summer a couple years ago before he went on his Mission."

"He's too old for Jennalee, isn't he?"

"Too old? No, they were supposed to get married after she graduated from high school. Then something got into her—she's so stubborn—and now I don't think she's going to."

Alex felt his face do a slow burn. "Isn't she free to decide?"

"Well, I know Bridger told her he'd wait for her for a while. Dad wants her to marry him because . . ."

"I'm listening," Alex said, hot behind his ears.

"Bridger's really smart and is going to BYU. His dad owns a huge business, and someday, Bridger will be the CEO."

"Oh," said Alex as a thousand knives struck him. A wave of self-pity knocked hope aside. He was a 'nobody' compared to Bridger. His own father had died with huge medical bills, no business; there was no inheritance. In Utah, he wouldn't count at all; he wasn't a Mormon, nor could he ever be a returned missionary.

He sauntered over to the rest rooms, got a drink out of the water fountain, and soberly waited for the girl he cared about. But a sense of alienation overpowered him. He wasn't a member of this club, and there was no use trying to be.

Her entire family now stood near the baggage claim, talking to Moab. The Townsend family did the same with Bridger, who stood tall in the center. Alex saw him scan the area. It was clear who he was looking for.

At last she came out, red-faced, hiding behind her hair. She'd been crying.

"It's all good," Alex said, "Boston told me about Bridger."

"I didn't know he'd be arriving at the same time as Moab, Alex, you've got to believe me. I didn't even realize it was time for him to come back. I broke it off with him."

Alex swallowed. "I believe you, but I'm in an awkward position right now, you know? Go say hello to your cousin, and I'll just wait over by the exit door, okay?"

"Come and shake Moab's hand. We can ignore the Townsends. They hate me anyway."

"Really, Jennalee, I think this is a 'family only' thing. I'll meet Moab some other time."

"Okay." She made a wide sweep around the room to reach her family, spent a few minutes there, and then hurried back to Alex.

He tried to look casual, leaning against a wall, avoiding the drama before him, his hopes deflated.

As he took Jennalee's arm to leave, the entire tribe of Townsends moved toward the same exit. Bridger, who'd been smiling, immediately took on a look of hurt when he spotted Jennalee. Alex saw the redhead's eyes narrow when he figured out that Jennalee was with another guy. Together, Alex and Jennalee pushed the revolving glass door hard, sweeping them out into the evening air, where they sprinted to the farthest parking garage.

■　■　■

"What exactly did Boston tell you about me and Bridger?" she asked after they got into her car. Alex's small pickup didn't have enough gas, so she'd said she would drive.

"Nothing much. Just that you went out with him for a whole summer and after you graduated, you were supposed to . . ."

"Get married? Well that's all off."

"Before or after you met me?" Alex tried not to sound ticked.

"About the same time we met."

"So you don't want to marry him?"

"Alex, I don't love him. He's got plenty of girls to choose from, and one of them will marry him in a minute. My brother Brent knows him well. They were roommates, and I trust what my brother says more than anyone. That's why I broke it off." Jennalee pulled on to the freeway north.

"Looks to me like Bridger has money, probably owns a sports car."

"He does have a BMW convertible, but believe it or not, I don't care about his stuff. Bridger is not for me. I can't be happy with him."

Alex probed. "His father's rich, has a business, which Bridger inherits. If you married him, you'd never lack for anything. Why are you passing that up?"

"Money isn't everything, Alex. I'm not going to get married until I choose to. I want to see the world, go to college and be like your mother, not mine."

"Why my mom?"

"She's independent and strong, has a PhD, and travels the world. That's my dream, and I want to at least have the choice to spread my wings."

Alex relaxed a bit. "Wow, you nailed it. Mom's a feisty Italian who says it like it is, and you *are* kind of like her."

"I almost fell into a trap, Alex. And I can't explain it, but I'm beginning to see life from your standpoint, and for the first time, I'm changing my thinking, moving in a different direction."

That surprised him. "Let me get this straight. You want to move in a different direction and to tell the truth, I like a more predictable life. Right now I'm living by the seat of my pants. Don't get me wrong, I trust God. I know He has a plan, but sometimes I wish my life was as planned out as yours. Nothing to go wrong that way."

She frowned. "But no freedom either. My life's definitely planned out, but the people who control it forgot to take me into consideration. I'm not ready to be tied down with children and a house. And I won't sacrifice my happiness to please my parents." Jennalee stared hard at the road through the heavy northbound traffic, her hands gripping the wheel. She'd long since quit crying, but her face was still pink.

"Your parents will think I had something to do with you changing your mind about Bridger, and he knows for sure I did, by his expression."

"I barely knew you then, but yes, you had a lot to do with changing my mind. So did my brother. You don't know what a breath of fresh air you are, Alex Campanaro! My parents think it's me, that I'm stubborn, so they won't blame you, not totally. And Brent's on my side."

Alex felt a tiny bit better. "So you want to travel. Jennalee, you're giving up the good life that guy can give you; he could take you all over the world, first class."

"Can't you see I want to be independent? I want to leave and never come back. For a while, anyway." Her pretty face oozed pure vulnerability. She really didn't know what the outside world was like, away from the safety of home.

He wanted to warn her about how lonely it was to be on the outside. "Jennalee, if you rebel completely, you'll be lost without your family. Don't burn any bridges that you won't be able to cross again."

Jennalee laughed in a giddy way. "Bridgers, you mean. I've already done that! I love my family, but I can't live an unhappy life, doing only what they want. Grandma Young's on my side. I've talked to her about it."

In silence, she parked the car in front of his house not far from the high school in Kaysville and turned off the engine. "I promised you'd be home for dinner, and here you are."

Alex sighed. Never had he known a girl like Jennalee Young. She wore no perfume, but an aura followed her, a charisma that other girls didn't have. Even upset, she maintained a dignified presence. At that moment he knew he couldn't live without her in his life. Was it only two months since they'd met? In that time, they'd been with each other every day, but he'd never kissed her.

There was too much against them, no hope for a future together, so he'd held back getting physical in any way other than holding hands. Now she told him she didn't want the life her Mormon family had planned for her; she wanted to be different. Maybe they would make it together after all.

"Jennalee, I . . ." Alex took off his safety belt, and then, in one smooth move, took her face into his hands and crowned her lips with a soft kiss. Before she could say or do anything, he got out of the car and went inside.

Chapter Eleven

Parents

In the morning, all Jennalee could think about was that kiss. Soft and pure, like none other she'd had, solidifying their relationship. There was no turning back. She prayed for a future with Alex, college first, and then marriage. Lost in the dream, Jennalee put a bagel in the toaster just as her mom came into the kitchen to make breakfast for the boys.

Her mother was in a confrontational mood. "Hope you slept well, because we need to discuss a few things."

"What is it, Mom?"

"Jennalee, I really like Alex. He's nice and I know he's smart, but I don't think you should be going out with him, and you know why. What kind of future can you have with him?"

Jennalee donned a calm mask. "Mom, I'm trying to help him because he just moved here. But I'm not going to lie to you; I do like him. He's been talking to the missionaries and maybe he'll be baptized soon."

"Sweetheart, I trust your choices, but I think you'd best stay away from him. Dad and I are sure he'll break your heart. And now Bridger Townsend is back. Honey, doesn't he mean anything to you?"

"I told you I broke it off with him. He's not in love with me, Mom, and I'm definitely not in love with him."

Her mother whipped a bowl of raw eggs harder. "Jennalee Eliza, your future is at stake. If you're not married soon, then you need to go to BYU to find someone. I'll talk to your father about this, but until then, I—"

"Got to go, Mom, I'm late!" Jennalee scurried out the door to avoid her mom's directive. She knew the next sentence might be something like, *I forbid you to go out with Alex.*

■　■　■

The same morning, Alex woke up to the smell of coffee. He and Jennalee were to meet for lunch during open campus, so he'd eat breakfast at home. Rounding the corner, he heard his mom and Gabe talking, so lingered in the hall, and although it was eavesdropping, he was compelled to hear what they were talking about.

"What's the gospel the Mormons believe, Mom?" Gabe asked.

"Like most religions, it has to do with what their Church says they have to do to get to heaven. For instance, they have to believe that the Book of Mormon is true. It's like their Bible."

"So their gospel is way different than ours? Ours is pretty simple: that Jesus died for our sins and when we accept his sacrifice and make him Lord of our lives, we gain eternal life. So is that what they think?"

Mom paused. "I think they believe something like that, but they add to it with Prophets, Apostles, temples, and ordinances. The gospel we practice is a close and tender relationship with the true Jesus. He is the Way, the Truth and the Life. Their religion has Jesus as one of the many characters in it, and second-best at that."

"It's confusing. They use the same words."

Mom paused to pour her coffee. "Here's what I want you to remember. The truth is in the Bible, and their foundation is not the Bible."

"But they're good people, Mom. You said so yourself. Aren't we all supposed to be good?"

"Being good will never save us. LDS are compelled to be good by the strictness of their religion, like the Jews in Jesus' time. They have a lot of do's and don'ts, but for us, we follow the Holy Spirit's leading once we know the Lord."

"So do Mormons know Jesus?"

"Some might. We can't judge these things. We're born-again when we believe in the fullness of Jesus, and that he is completely one with God the Father. To be saved we rely on that grace relationship with him, not on good works or fulfilling rules and rituals. Jesus is all we need to get to heaven."

Alex chose this moment to enter the kitchen and put some bread in the toaster. It was hard to pretend he hadn't heard the conversation. "We're talking about what Mormons believe and what we believe," said Gabe.

Alex shrugged. "Yeah, I heard."

His mom got jelly out of the fridge and handed it to him. "I can't find the card with the missionaries' phone number on it. Do you know where it is?"

Alex watched his toast pop up and buttered it. "Sorry, I forgot. I think it's in my truck. I used it to call them, and they met with me and Jennalee in the park a few times."

His mother's face became troubled. "Alex, this isn't good. I want to talk to them myself, as the head of this family, with you and Gabe in the room. Were you able to share your own beliefs with them?"

"I'm trying, Mom, but it's kind of hard with three of them there."

She looked alarmed. "Well, of course it is. There's powerful pressure on you. Have they talked to you about getting baptized?"

"I'm not going to do it. Jennalee doesn't say much about it. I know she wants me to, but I just can't."

"Alex, please don't talk to them again without speaking to Pastor Ron about it, okay?" She took his face in her hands like the Italian mother she was and gazed at him. "And study the Word every day."

"Hey, I'm not that influenced," he told her, hiding the confusion preying on his mind. His mother was right. He was unsettled about his own beliefs when he'd never been that way before. He was attracted to their good, solid way of life and craved a sense of belonging among a group of awesome people. He was tired of being an outsider. And then there was Jennalee.

"We're all influenced, just living in Utah. I'm praying about your relationship with Jennalee. I want you to know that, son."

"I hope you're not praying against us, Mom."

"Never would I pray against any person. I like Jennalee. I pray you will both know what God wants for you. But let's face it, Alex, dating an LDS girl is a challenge you need to be prepared for. You have to know what you believe. The missionaries can convince even the strongest Bible-believing, born-again Christ-followers that they are right."

Alex chafed at her comment. "Got to go, Mom. No worries, I'll be fine." He didn't want to cause his mom concern, not after all she'd been through.

"Remember how you became stronger in the Lord through Dad's death? Don't weaken now. Talk to Pastor Ron."

"I will, Mom. I was thinking about calling him today," he answered truthfully. Pastor Ron could surely help with some of his confusion.

"Hold on. Before you go, I want you to know about a new development in my life. I've been reacquainted with a friend who your dad and I knew at Aviano Air Force Base in Italy. His name is Carl."

Shaken, Alex glanced at Gabe, who showed zero emotion. He tried to do the same. "So you're going out with him?"

"Yes," said his mother without skipping a beat, "and I'd like you to meet him Saturday night for dinner here. It's important to me, okay?"

Both boys promised to be home.

■　■　■

Alex saw Jennalee in the snowplowed parking lot of the high school. Driving was perilous that morning as a foot of snow had piled up overnight. He was a little reluctant to talk, because he knew he had to tell her he couldn't see the missionaries anymore. Not that he minded much, because if he admitted the truth, he was only doing listening to them for her sake. Her joyful face greeted him and he hurried toward her.

As they sauntered down the white-covered sidewalk, he took her hand. He spotted Madeline walking in their direction, also holding hands with a guy. They all said, "Hi," their breath lingering in the cold mist, as they passed one another.

"Wow," said Jennalee, "she looks great. I see she's moved on."

"You never believed we were just friends. Still are."

"Oh, Alex, I wish we were graduated, out of high school, and going to Weber State together."

"Me, too," he said, hoping nothing would change and their future plans really would take place.

But he knew change was inevitable. His mom had found a new man. His picture of the future clouded up like his warm breath in the frosty air. Alex stopped for a minute to tie his shoe with reddened fingers. He'd forgotten gloves in his haste to escape his mom's disquieting news and discussion on Mormonism. How could he keep this girl he was going with when they faced such obstacles? No matter, he had to try.

"Jenn, I started reading the Book of Mormon."

She looked pleased, and he almost hesitated to continue. "I ran into a weird thing. The Book called Alma says Jesus was born in Jerusalem. Even Christmas carols say he was born in Bethlehem, and that agrees with the Bible."

"Ask the missionaries," she replied. "I'm sure there's an answer, because the Book of Mormon has no mistakes, Alex. It's the most correct book ever translated."

"Hey, I wanted to ask you something else," he said, holding back because he knew he'd disappoint her. Winter wind tore at his coat. "Can you call the missionaries and tell them I can't make it today?"

She let go of his hand in the freezing wind, and he put it into his coat pocket.

Jennalee was quiet a moment. "You don't want to talk to them anymore? You don't think our Church is true, do you?"

"You don't understand what I think," he answered, welling up with anger. "You've always been told what to think and never how to figure things out for yourself."

Jennalee stopped in her tracks. "Alex, that's it; it's over. You can go out with Madeline now. At least she's not a Mormon." She practically ran to get ahead of him on the sidewalk.

He shouted, "What's over? Us, or the conversation?"

"Both." She whirled around, and stood in front of him, trembling.

"Jenn, talk to me," he said, in a low voice. "I don't want to go out with Madeline or anyone else. I care about you too much for us to be over. I never want to stop talking to you, even if it's about hard things like religion." Soft words turned away wrath, didn't they? And he meant them.

She took a deep breath and let it out slow. "What are we going to do, Alex?" She walked beside him again, and they stopped in front of the glass doors of the high school. It was time to separate until after school.

"Aren't we meeting for lunch?" he asked.

"Not now."

"Jenn, come over to my house after practice, okay?" Alex begged.

"About five, then," she said tersely.

■   ■   ■

Alex opened the screen door for Jennalee. "C'mon in. Mom needed my truck. Her car's in the shop, so I can't pick you up tomorrow. Sorry." The whole day he'd been alone, without her. She hadn't texted him once. Now she was on his doorstep, looking away from him, uncomfortable.

"I can pick you up tomorrow," she said, "no problem."

"That'd be great. Make yourself at home. I'll get you something to eat." She sat on the couch as Alex grabbed the remote and switched the TV off. He went into the kitchen, returning with a tray of cheese and crackers. "You're probably hungry after cheering practice."

"Way hungry, thanks. Listen, Alex, I may as well tell you I'm hurt you don't want to see the missionaries anymore. I guess I thought you might . . . but I'm trying to understand, I really am."

"You wanted me to convert, Jenn, and I can't. I've thought about this all day. Can we find some middle ground with our faiths so we can keep seeing each other? Because I want to stay together."

She took a cracker and put cheese on top. "Me, too. I'll admit I dated you at first because I was tired of all the boys I'd known from Primary and wanted someone different, more exciting. I didn't know my feelings about you would grow as much as they have."

Sounded like their relationship must matter to her as much as it did to him. Her intention in going out with him wasn't only a rebellious fling. A new paradigm was opening with Jennalee, an honest one.

"So why don't you want to join the Church?" she asked.

"Because I know it's not about any church. It's about a real relationship with Jesus."

"What does that mean in practice, Alex? You can't skip church, disobey the Ten Commandments; you can't throw out the baby with the bath water," Jennalee retorted, surprising him in her vehemence.

"To me the word *church* means all people worldwide who love Jesus and follow him, not a building or a denomination. If we believe He died for our sins, accept his Lordship over our lives, hand over our will to him and align ourselves with the New Testament, that's all we need to do. That's the gospel in a nutshell."

"I believe all that."

"What I'm trying to explain, and I'm not very good at it, is that there's something deeper than any man-made religion on earth. It's an individual true relationship with our Creator."

"I've heard about being born-again, Alex, and I have an opinion."

"Let's hear it," he said, prompting her, but a little nervous about what she might say.

"Wait a minute, you sound irritated with me."

Alex sighed. "I'm not, Jennalee, but I have an opinion, too. Latter-day Saints like to put us born-agains in a box. You think we're nice and have good values, and we're even righteous, but you put us down by not hearing what we have to say."

"You know why?" She crossed her arms in a defensive gesture. "We *can't* listen to you, Alex, because unbelief will creep into our faith, and it's dangerous." She sounded afraid.

"So you're not allowed to doubt what you've been told all your life? Or research it? Have you ever looked at the origins of your religion?"

Her eyes narrowed. "Is that what you've been doing?"

"Yes, I have. The missionaries mentioned some things that I had to research."

"I see. Well, what about you? As a born-again Christian, do you nurse doubts or do detective work into your own faith? I mean, if you did, you'd find the Bible hasn't been translated correctly."

"I'm going to leave that comment alone. Don't you see, Jennalee? If we really want any kind of long-term relationship, we have to learn to discuss things without attitude."

Her chin lifted. "Now you tell me I have an attitude problem?"

Alex held his calm demeanor. In a quiet voice, he said, "I have a question. Are you afraid of finding out whether your doubts could be true?"

A long second passed. "No."

"How can you allow the religion that you were born into the final say for your whole life? You owe it to yourself to re-examine it with adult understanding. I know we're in Utah, but the rest of the world doesn't center on Mormonism."

She let loose tears now. Maybe he'd gone too far. "How can you say that? You don't understand. We do have doubts, all the time. We have to go to the bishop and get prayer and blessings from the priesthood holders. If we stop believing," she choked on the word, "if we lose our faith, then we lose everything. Everything!" She plopped onto the couch. Tears dripped in twos from her chin, and Alex handed her a tissue.

He looked at her. "Jenn, this isn't a fight between *us*. It's about our beliefs. *They're* against each other; we're not. Listen, you're an amazing person and . . ."

"Do you hate Mormons, Alex, like everyone else?"

"No, I love a Mormon, and she's sitting on my couch."

She tried to hide her smile under the tissue, but he saw it—a slight, warm sparkle.

He continued. "Words can't explain it. There's mystery in God that no one can make into a doctrine: it's who God really is. If everything was so cut and dried, and had easy answers, we wouldn't be totally dependent on God. We'd become people-pleasing pew sitters."

"I'll think about it, but I find all the born-again stuff cut and dried, too," she said. "LDS doctrine has the answers by revelation and that's all we need."

"I know, I know. They have an answer for everything."

"Now *you* have an attitude problem."

"All I'm saying is, if you know Jesus, he shows you what a relationship with God looks like. It's the truth."

"So now you have a corner on the truth?"

"I think the LDS people are the best ever, but I want intellectual freedom to doubt and ask questions. Because truth is the most important thing to find in life."

"I can't doubt what my Church teaches!"

"I'm not asking you to. But when you do, try finding answers in the Bible."

She sniffed and exhaled. "Part of me wants freedom to decide what to do with my life, maybe even freedom to doubt. A big part of me is confused about who's right and who's wrong."

A tea kettle whistled and Alex held a finger up. "Hold that thought." He went to the kitchen and hurried back with two mugs of hot chocolate. "Jenn, it must be awful to doubt the religion you grew up with. But in the end, you don't lose, you gain."

She wrapped her hands around the steaming mug and took a sip. "I know what we should do, okay? Let's not talk about religion for a while. I'll stop proselytizing you, and you stop proselytizing me." Her back was straight and tense, and she'd stopped crying.

The air deflated from his lungs. He'd wracked his brains to explain the true Good News to her without seeming to proselytize. But now he'd have to give her time to think about it. "How about if I read the Book of Mormon and you read the New Testament? We'll discuss the common things we find in them."

"Okay. And we need to be calm about discussing Scriptures."

"Jenn, the other thing we have to face is that our families aren't happy about us. Yours find you an LDS guy if I disappear for even a day."

She stood, pausing for almost a minute. Then she looked at him, her eyes sparkling and clear. "I don't want an LDS guy, Alex. You know something? Our common ground is that we not only like each other, we're heading toward loving each other."

Alex put down his mug and rushed to take her in his arms to kiss her.

Chapter Twelve
Pride, Prejudice, and Persecution

"Please come, Alex. It's important to my entire family, and I want you there." They walked together to the parking lot after school the week before Thanksgiving.

"Are you sure?" Alex winced at the thought of being around her family again. With them, he was in the wrong skin. Now she begged him to go to her maternal grandparents' 50th Wedding Anniversary celebration with every family member who wasn't on a Mission.

"They're doing all the temple stuff the day before, so there'll be nothing religious about it, only the celebration on the farm in Heber City. I'll drive."

"Okay, on one condition."

"What?"

"That you go out with me tomorrow, to a movie."

She laughed. "Easy. You know I love movies. That's a given."

"I wasn't sure we were as close after our discussion the other day."

"I'm okay about it, Alex, as long as we keep to the non-proselytizing pact. Just read and discuss common Scriptures."

"Okay," he said, taking her hand, "fill me in on who'll be attending. I can't remember too many names once I get there."

"My mom has only two siblings, my Uncle Roy and Aunt Katie. Uncle Roy is married to Marie, and they have nine children on their farm."

"Did you say nine?"

"Right. Now Aunt Katie married a guy named Ethan Coombs, and they have seven kids. Those are the basics, but my grandparents have siblings, too, and several will be there, only you don't have to pay too much attention to that generation."

Whew, thought Alex, meeting her folks at the airport was one hurdle he'd jumped. Now there were more. Imagine the questions these people would pepper him with, especially showing up as Jennalee's boyfriend. "Will your Grandma Young be there?"

"I know she's invited. She usually comes to these things, but it's not the Young side of the family, you know."

"I hope she comes. I can always talk to her. What should I say about not being LDS?"

"They won't ask. I mainly want you to see the farm where my mom grew up. We can be outside with the kids most of the time. We'll leave early, and go Christmas shopping at the outlet stores in Park City."

He took a deep breath. "Okay, I'd love to see the farm and meet your mom's side. But shopping? Do I have to?"

"My brothers hate shopping, too. I don't care if you sit and watch people while I shop. Oh, and we have to dress in Sunday best for the party, if you don't mind."

He shrugged, giving in to it all just to be with her.

■　■　■

Saturday came, and Jennalee picked him up in her car. After a breezy ride up the mountains to the west, they arrived at the remote community of Heber City. A mile away, the family farm's fields lay neatly fallow. Every fence was painted white, there was no rusty equipment in tall weeds, no ramshackle barns with mossy roofs. It was a story-book farm: a sprawling white house with a wrap-around porch, a trampoline in the back yard, gardens with pumpkins on the vines, and trees with tire swings.

"One's for the big kids and the other's for the little kids," Jennalee explained.

Except for the 1960s sunken living room, the house was updated with granite countertops and hickory cabinets, thick new carpet and a stone fireplace. On the gnarled juniper mantelpiece stood a plaque with a warm message: *Families Are Forever.*

Alex had seen this common slogan all over Utah. Family was important, but the mantra disturbed him a little. To him, family was a side benefit of heaven, but not the main event.

Jennalee's relatives showed him sincere kindness, and she was right; there were no questions asked, not yet anyway. He tried to count the children in the house, porch, patio, yard, and barn, but never got a full count on moving targets. It was like a gigantic wedding reception rather than an anniversary. There was even a wedding cake, a photo booth, tables brimming with food and a Western band.

"My Grandpa's friends play old music, and I mean old," Jennalee told him, "so let's leave early."

"It might be fun to dance to it. Square dance, I mean."

"Ooh, not for me." She looked at him like he was crazy.

"It was a joke, Jennalee. I hate square dancing, too, ever since I got stuck with Marylou Winsted as a partner in fifth grade."

"Square dancing scarred you for life?" She laughed. "C'mon, let's go see the barn."

Huge wooden spools were set up in the barn as tables, and a number of women and children sat on hay bales. Propane heaters warmed up the space, where about twenty children filled paper plates with food as though they hadn't eaten for some time. A glass punch bowl with floating lemons and piles of meat and cheese for sandwiches sat in the middle of one of the spools. Alex helped himself to a sandwich, and Jennalee dipped a cup in the punch.

"Aren't you going to introduce us to your young man, Jennalee?"

Alex saw her startle and look around. A gray-haired man came out of the shadows where he'd been talking to another man. "Oh, Uncle Levi, I didn't see you. This is my friend from school, Alex Campanaro."

"Pleasure, Alex. Don't recall ever meeting you, but we did meet her other feller. Who was your other boyfriend, Jennalee?" The man grinned the way a fox would.

Jumping up from her place on a hay bale, a plump woman, dressed in a satiny blue dress under a sweater, sidled her way next to Uncle Levi. "It was Bridger Townsend, wasn't it? I'm Ellen, by the way. Glad to meet any friend of Jennalee's." She shook Alex's hand.

"And I'm Elizabeth, Ellen's sister," said a woman in a plaid coat, holding a baby in a blanket. "Nice to meet you." They looked like twins.

Another man leaned in a corner, one boot on the wall, watching them like a spider stalks a fly, saying nothing. Jennalee's face looked tense.

"Well, I'm no longer going with Bridger. This is Alex, and I'm showing him around Grandpa's farm. We're on our way outside to the tire swing. Want to come, Rylee?" A cute girl in a tiny pink dress looked up from her paper plate.

"Can I?" she asked, looking at the two women.

Ellen responded, "Say 'May I?' first, Rylee."

The little girl complied.

"Yes, you may, but get your jacket on. It's cold out there."

The clipped, harsh way she said it to the little girl made Alex wince.

Jennalee took the child's hand and practically shoved Alex out of the barn before he could hear Uncle Levi say, "One of those city types, definitely not from Zion. What do you think, Ethan, did you see his fancy suit and leather shoes?"

■　■　■

Pushing Logan on the tire swing, Jennalee seemed carefree about what had happened in the barn. But even on this cool November day, Alex saw perspiration bead on her forehead and a serious look on her face.

"Are you going to tell me what that was all about?" Alex whispered into her ear. "I think I've figured it out, but who's Uncle Levi?"

"My grandpa's half-brother. I didn't know he'd be here. He's family and we love him, but he's gone off the deep end."

"How? Polygamy?" Though whispered, there it was, the word was out, lingering in the air between them. The invisible elephant living in Utah was exposed in all of its caked mud and complicated wrinkles of skin.

Jennalee wiped her forehead with her hand and pushed the tire harder with the other one. "Not too loud, Alex," she murmured, "some of the kids don't understand."

Logan's turn ended, and they helped him off. Alex lifted Rylee up to the tire to put her skinny legs through. "Polyg!" shouted Logan into her face, before sprinting to the house. In an instant, Jennalee had kicked off her high heels and run after him, tackling him on the leaf-covered grass.

"Don't you ever call her that, do you hear me? She can't help it," she shouted at him. "I'm going to tell Dad."

"Please don't," Logan cried.

"You have to apologize and kiss her shoe in front of all the kids," Jennalee said with a self-righteousness Alex hadn't seen before.

"Kiss her shoe?" Logan sighed. "Okay, just don't tell Dad I said that word."

His face wrinkled in fear on the way back to the swing where he had to carry out Jennalee's cruel and unusual punishment. Alex could see that for Logan, it was the ultimate humiliation. Still sitting in her thin hoodie in the tire, Rylee giggled at the princess treatment.

"Is that why Uncle Levi's kids weren't in the house but in the barn?" Alex asked.

Jennalee gave him an infuriated look. "I guess you noticed they're kind of persecuted because the family's divided about it. Logan heard that awful word from one of the other cousins. Our family never says it."

Alex loosened his tie. It was going to be a long afternoon. "I'm going to the house to get something to drink and find Grandma Young."

"She didn't come, but I'll be there in a minute." She stared straight ahead, pushing the swing for Rylee.

■ ■ ■

From the wrap-around porch, he watched her escort Rylee back to the barn. Then she walked slowly towards the house, swinging her shoes in one hand.

"Got you some lemonade."

"Thanks." She was quiet as she sat down on a chair.

"Who's the other guy in there, Jennalee? Another polygamist?"

She took a deep breath. "It's my Uncle Ethan. He's married to my mom's sister, Katie, remember?"

Alex didn't, but he wasn't going to say.

"Aunt Katie's been upset lately about Ethan getting friendly with Uncle Levi. He used to be a lot nicer and look at him now. He didn't even say 'hi'."

"I noticed. He's probably getting into polygamy himself. What guy wouldn't?"

Jennalee stared at him, frowning. "Alex, I'm surprised at you. You have to understand that plural marriage was a calling, it wasn't from human lust. It was God's command."

"Right, well, that's a little hard for me to believe. It's not in the Ten Commandments last I checked." Then he saw her face. "I know that's what you believe, but it doesn't sit right with me. And I don't think it sits right with you, either."

She shook her head slowly. "Actually, I heard Mom talking to Aunt Katie on the phone, and she doesn't believe Ethan is being called by God to do this. It's against what our Apostles say nowadays. He could be excommunicated."

"So what does your dad think?"

"Dad's mainline LDS through and through. See, Uncle Levi married Ellen twelve years ago after he divorced his first wife. That was okay, but Ellen brought her sister Elizabeth in after a year or two. Then, another wife. I think her name's Tina, and there's one named Kimber, too. It's terrible, because Uncle Levi's at least sixty, and his last wife is barely twenty."

Alex didn't know what to say, so he tried to lighten it up. "What man wouldn't want four pretty women seeing to his every want?" He saw disgust on her face. "Except me, of course. I'm no dirty old man."

"Don't say that, Alex. I know he's out of line, but he shouldn't be persecuted, should he? Especially by his own family. Our people have had enough persecution."

"What about Rylee and all the kids? They get persecuted by other kids and never get much attention."

"You're wrong. They get plenty of attention from the sister wives and siblings, believe me. Rylee belongs to Elizabeth. She's my favorite."

He took a long sip of punch. "I can see why; she's really sweet." He'd never been this uncomfortable with Jennalee but he had to say what he was thinking. "That means some of the kids are brothers and sisters and cousins all at once. Complicated."

She shrugged. "At least they have a lot of playmates."

He refilled his cup with lemonade, downed it, and filled it again. What he really needed was a cup of java to get him through this conversation. He almost laughed. Coffee was forbidden, but four wives? Not exactly.

■　　■　　■

After good-byes and hugs, with photos posted immediately on a private family website, Alex and Jennalee drove to Park City. The fresh air of the mountain town revived him. How could such bizarre practices exist in a land that looked like God's country? The whole subject of polygamy was foreign and strange.

They'd been quiet on the way there, when Jennalee finally said, "I know you're shocked about my family."

"Not shocked, really, but I pity the kids, especially Rylee. She's skinny, and her clothes weren't warm enough," Alex said. "How can men want a life that causes suffering for their children? Not to mention the wives?"

"Everyone tries to help. We give them our old clothes. That pink dress was my cousin's."

"I'm sorry, Jenn, but I have to say what I think. Your Uncle Levi is a letch."

She flinched. "God commanded people to 'be fruitful and multiply.' And look at Abraham and Jacob in the Bible. Even David and Solomon had multiple wives."

"Those guys got themselves into loads of trouble by having too many wives, and it's all outlined for everyone to see how they disobeyed God's warnings. But, hey, I thought the Bible wasn't translated correctly, so why would you use it to excuse polygamy?"

Surprise grazed Jennalee's face, but she recovered. "Oh, Alex, get off your soapbox. I only recently learned about this history in Seminary. I admit there are some hard things in our Church history. Brigham Young himself had quite a few wives."

"I noticed. I was downtown last week with my mom. Did you ever take a look at those window gables upstairs in Lion House? Little bedrooms all in a row—twelve on the west and twelve on the east. Twenty-four wives right there. Not to mention the ones he had working on his farm."

"You've been reading all this stuff somewhere, haven't you? You can't believe all the Mormon bashing on the internet." She was calm as ever. "My grandfather and the other prophets took the Bible as an example and God commanded them to practice it for the good of the faith and community."

"Okay, but now you say the main Church doesn't accept it."

"Right, the Church doesn't recognize polygamists as true Mormons. But polygamy is recognized as God-ordained for the times it was practiced. It was a revelation for that time. It also took care of widows and orphans."

"So let me ask you this: do *you* want to end up like Ellen, Elizabeth, Tina, and Kimberley?"

"Kimber. No, I don't. Why would you even ask?"

"Because I . . ."

"Alex, as a woman, I know how hard it would be to live out. Women who enter into it have to be sweet and obedient."

"Sounds like you, Jennalee."

"Very funny. No way am I that obedient. Ask my dad. The main thing is, I think Uncle Levi is out of line because he can't afford those kids. My grandparents are upset about that very thing."

"How many does he have?"

"I don't even know. I only know Elizabeth's six kids, and a few of Ellen's. Tina just had a baby and Kimber's too new."

He could see she was conflicted about this, and wondered what his friend Tony would say. Because her family was so kind to him, guilt pangs hit him hard. But he wanted to ask someone else, someone who had lived here a long time. He could see how convoluted it was, with most LDS people disapproving, and some looking the other way.

Jennalee adjusted her shopping bag as they walked from store to store. "It's no longer against state law."

"You're kidding. Oh, I get it, because of the guy on TV with his wives. Didn't he have a lawsuit?"

"Yes, and he won, based on freedom of religion. Only they call it co-habitation. I found out that it's still in Doctrines and Covenants, Section 132, even though the manifesto put an end to it in 1890."

"That makes everything even more ambiguous." Alex laughed to dull the tension. "You sound like you read all this every day."

Jennalee swatted at him. "Let's go. I think I've hit all my favorite stores."

They got in the car. Alex sighed, "So to some guys, it must look like heaven on earth to have all those wives."

"Heaven on earth? I guess so. In heaven, some men will have more than one wife. I mean if they're sealed in the temple. Like if one dies and he gets married again, or . . ."

Alex whistled. "So polygamy is in your heaven?" That must be what the *Families Are Forever* signs meant. He couldn't stand it anymore, he had to think about something else. "Hey, Jennalee, see that ice cream place? Let's get some; I need it to process this."

■ ■ ■

Tony came over Sunday afternoon to shoot some hoops in Gabe's new basketball hoop. The sun made the day warm, even though Thanksgiving approached. Alex told him about his encounter the day before. "I couldn't believe it. There can't be much polygamy left since it was outlawed, and here it is in Jennalee's family!"

"I'm not surprised one bit," Tony said, sounding wise. "Joseph Smith had thirty-some wives. Brigham Young, fifty-some. It's entrenched in their belief system, even if they don't actually practice it." Tony bounced the ball a few times. "I should show you something. Let's go for a ride. I'll buy you a hamburger on the way."

"Okay, as long as it's not two hot dogs for a dollar," Alex teased.

After eating their burgers, they drove around the foothills of the Wasatch front, where massive mansions hugged the hillsides.

Tony pointed out a colossal house. "See the one with five garages and the little kid toys on the balcony? It's owned by a polygamist."

"No way, *here*? Aren't they all hiding on remote farms or on the Arizona border? How can they be right here in the suburbs of Salt Lake?"

"It's an open secret. Remember, this is Davis County, where the Kingston clan lives. They're one of the largest polygamous sects in Utah. Nobody bothers them unless they're doing something openly abusive. And that's rare."

Staring, Alex saw a woman pull out of the driveway in a car that looked like a Lexus. Two baby seats were strapped in the back. He thought of Rylee's poverty. So this is the other side of polygamy.

Tony kept talking. "There's a suburb west of Provo called Eagle Mountain. The plural wives have their own houses there, but they all belong to the same ward." He took the ramp back to Kaysville.

"How do you know all this?" Alex asked.

"I've lived here all my life, and I read the newspaper. Rich polygamists can take care of the women and kids, so they're pretty much free to do what they want. They believe the highest heaven is reserved for them because Joseph Smith said so. Some think the mainline LDS will miss the boat."

"And vice versa from what Jennalee said about her dad. Listen, I can't imagine my mom going for something like this."

"Your mom was never LDS. That's what I'm trying to explain to you about Mormon girls. They're raised with these beliefs and history, and they don't question religious authorities. No doubts allowed."

"Jennalee's different, Tony. She doesn't go for this, either, she told me. She's independent. I mean, she's going out with me, isn't she? It's brave of her, when I think about it."

Tony shrugged. "She's dating you now, but we'll see how long before the pressure gets to her."

Chapter Thirteen
Growth and Change

He didn't stay long, this new friend of their mother's. Mom made chicken *piccata* with capers and mushrooms. After they ate and talked a while, the balding gray-haired man left in his BMW. He didn't want to play basketball.

Gabe and Alex washed pots as Mom cleaned the counters. "Thank you guys for being so polite to Carl. It means a lot to me."

"It's cool Dad knew him, too," said Gabe with enthusiasm. "They even worked at the Base together."

"Yes. Carl's a little older than Dad was, so they weren't that close, but they knew each other." She stood in the kitchen with a dish towel, a forlorn look on her face. "I'm really trying to move on, guys."

Alex, seeing her distress, put his arm around her in a side hug. "It's okay with us, Mom. Carl's a nice guy, and we can tell he makes you happy, huh, Gabe?"

His brother nodded.

"You two are the best sons I could ever have had. Carl and I are taking things slow. We're not jumping into anything. Meanwhile, let's talk about you, Alex."

"More love talk," said Gabe, "I'm out of here." He ditched the kitchen for the living room, turning up the volume on the TV.

She handed Alex another piece of cheesecake. "You seem genuinely happy with Jennalee."

"Yeah, I am."

"So where are you in your relationship?" She sounded more worried than stern.

"I don't know," he began. "I mean, I seriously like her."

"I trust you when it comes to being a gentleman because I know you. You're like your dad."

"Thanks, Mom. I hope so. I don't want to add to your stress."

"What I really want to talk about is Jennalee is LDS, a belief system very different than yours. Do you think there's a future with her?"

"I think so. I hope so," he said, hearing the vagueness in his voice. "We've talked about going to the same college."

His mom let out a deep sigh. "When we moved to Utah, I thought something like this could happen, but I hoped you'd find a girl at our church."

"Mom, it's okay, we decided not to talk about religion, and we're not seeing the missionaries anymore."

"Have you talked about marriage?"

"She doesn't want to get married until after college, and I'm the same way. We'd like to travel and get good jobs."

"Alex, you know how I feel about dating. It's serious. You need to choose someone you could end up married to—no random dating, with no purpose."

"Mom, I could marry Jennalee."

Another sigh from his tired mom. "It would be an uphill battle for both of you. You have totally different cultural backgrounds and world views, all mixed in with religion."

"I know," Alex said, hot all of a sudden. "But weren't you and Dad in the same boat? He was from America; you were from Italy."

"Yes," said his mom, "that's why I know what I'm talking about. We were so much in love that I thought it would be easy, but marriage is work. I hate to see you start out with all those issues."

Alex looked outside the window. "I seriously like Jennalee, Mom. So whatever happens, we have to handle it."

"All I'm saying is, don't let things get too serious and jeopardize your future."

"You said you trusted me, Mom." Alex reluctantly faced her.

"I do, but when feelings are strong . . ."

"Please, Mom, stop worrying. I'm going to watch TV with Gabe." He didn't mean to leave abruptly, but he could see her getting worked up over nothing. On the couch, he stared at people on the TV screen and thought hard. He knew Mom tried her best to parent alone, and she constantly missed her husband, his dad. He didn't want to hurt her, but he knew what he was doing.

His cell phone buzzed. It was Jennalee.

■　　■　　■

Alex tried to keep his voice down. "I thought we agreed not to discuss doctrines."

"I'm not, but I had to ask this one question." said Jennalee. "I was listening to a guy on the car radio named Charles Stanley. He has a Southern accent."

"Charles Stanley is as well-known to me as Thomas Monson is to you. What did he say?"

"That it's only by the grace of Jesus that we're saved. No one is perfect enough to go to heaven without Jesus. But I know it takes more than that."

"More than Jesus and God's grace?"

"The Book of Mormon says grace comes in only 'after all we can do,'" she said, pronouncing each word slowly, "but Charles Stanley says grace covers all. No one has to even try to be good? Why not just fall into sin, confess it, and then sin again?"

"Christ-followers would call that cheap grace, Jennalee, and you're right, some people take advantage of it. But grace cost Jesus his life. If we honestly love the Lord, we can't keep sinning. It grieves him because we're disregarding the blood that saved us."

"LDS know how to confess and get rid of sin."

"We do, too, but ours isn't under the auspices of an institution. We confess directly to God. When we surrender our will to God, he helps us."

"It's so confusing. Doesn't free grace stop people from trying to model themselves on Jesus and even from doing good works? If you don't need works to get to heaven, why do any?"

"Paul the Apostle explains it really well in the Epistles. If you have a true relationship with Jesus, you love him so much that good works just pour out of you."

There was a pause, then: "I sort of get that, but it's too simple, Alex. We have to do *something* for grace. Don't you have to do *anything* to deserve it?"

Alex changed the cell to his other ear. The two of them were talking in a circle again. "Give me a minute, let me look it up . . . here it is in Ephesians 2:8 and 9: 'For it is by grace you have been saved, through faith—and this is not from yourselves, it is the gift of God—not by works, so that no one can boast.'"

"But there has to be more to it. We have to be baptized and go to Sacrament. We confess to the bishop. And what about the temple ordinances? Without those, we can't get to Celestial Heaven."

"Think about it, and we'll talk later," said Alex. "I'm tired, and I still have to study for a test tomorrow."

■　■　■

That night, Alex gazed at the white-covered Wasatch Mountains. Voicing the truth about Jennalee to his mom discouraged him. The powerful network of the majority religion in Utah might defeat their relationship from continuing. His visit to the local ward chapel, talking to the missionaries, reading the Book of Mormon, meeting her family; all that was only the tip of the iceberg. The sheer size and organization of the Church stood against any future together.

The Bible said that you'd know them by their fruits, and from his perspective, he saw a lot of good fruit from the Mormons. Their benevolence committees helped a lot of people. No one from his own church helped his family move into their rental house after they'd lived in a motel for weeks. But in his neighborhood, he noticed LDS men helping each other move furniture, plant lawns, and build fences and sheds. They were an amazing group.

With such confusing thoughts, sleep was random and half-awake.

In the morning, before coffee, his first impression was what he should've done from the start: to go see Pastor Ron. The missionaries had a good answer for every question he asked them. Would Pastor Ron?

Chapter Fourteen
The Way, The Truth, and The Life

"Hey, Alex," said Pastor Ron. He offered a comfortable chair in a direct line across from his desk. Near the phone, Alex noticed a smooth river rock with colorful painting that said, "Jesus is the Way, the Truth, and the Life," as well as a framed picture of his wife, toddler, and baby.

"I've got some major questions, Pastor. I don't want to be out of God's will, but I'm going with an LDS girl, and I need answers."

Pastor Ron nodded. "Not an unusual dilemma here in Utah, Alex. Go ahead, tell me about it."

"My mom thinks dating someone you can't actually marry isn't right. So can a marriage work when people are different faiths? Jennalee may not be able to change her religion for me."

"Have you looked into the Bible for answers?"

"I can't find the right Scriptures," Alex said, "and I'm mixed up about what the missionaries told me."

"That would do it alright. No wonder you're confused. We have a lot of ex-Mormons in our church. Would it help if you talked to someone who was once LDS?"

"I think so. They'd know a lot about this, but my question to you is: does it matter that much if we're not the same religion?"

"It matters because the Bible says you shouldn't be unequally yoked with an unbeliever. You shouldn't marry anyone who doesn't truly know and walk with Jesus."

"That's my problem. I think she is a believer. We talk about Jesus a lot. They're good people with good values, and sometimes they're better than us evangelicals. Our LDS neighbors shoveled the snow in our driveway yesterday before I was even up."

"They are good people, but good works don't save any of us. By the way, my wife used to be LDS."

"She did?"

"Yes, and her change was gradual, a long process where she asked lots of questions and studied the origins of the LDS Church. Eventually, she came out of that heritage and found a new one in the real Jesus Christ."

"The *real* Jesus?"

"The LDS understanding of Jesus is totally different than ours, Alex. We believe that Jesus is the Son of God, and that he has a Divine Nature. To them, Jesus is an exalted man. They think he is our brother who worked his way up to become a god with a small *g*."

"I've heard that, but they call Him 'Our Savior' or 'Son of God', the same words we use."

"I know, but their understanding of those words is different. To them, Jesus is a Pattern for us to follow to achieve heaven. But if he's only a *created* being who was really, really good, there was no need for him to defeat sin and save us by dying on the Cross."

"Okay," said Alex, "what about Heavenly Father? They talk about him a lot."

"He's a separate person to them, also a created being who can't be everywhere at the same time. Our Father in Heaven is Triune: Father God, the Son, and the Holy Spirit, who always existed, who is omnipresent and knows all. He's a big God, the Lord of Lords, and He loves us, hears our prayers, and knows our every thought. He is Spirit, not flesh."

"Wow, I'll have to study the Bible more. I like the Gospel of John, so I'm going to read it again."

"Do that, because you live in a foreign land now, Alex. Look at Ephesians, Colossians, and Romans, too. The Living Word of God will go straight into your Spirit and drive out confusion."

"So do you think it's okay if I go out with Jennalee? It's hard to know God's will."

"Listen, Alex. God's will is always to seek and save people. If you totally align your mind and will with His, if you trust in Jesus and follow Him, you're in His will. But stay in the Word."

"I can see I need to pray more, too. Set me up to talk to an ex-Mormon. You've given me a lot to think about, Pastor, thanks." Just as Alex began to leave the office, curiosity got the better of him. "So if your wife used to be Mormon, did you date her while she was one?"

Pastor Ron's face softened. "Yes, but that's a story for another day."

Chapter Fifteen
The Argentinean Soccer Boys

Nightmares from what he'd seen in the slums haunted Brent at night, though he never spoke of it to Ammon, his companion. They rose together at daybreak to study the LDS Scriptures, looking for some insight they'd missed. Spending so much time in these Scriptures, he became curious about the passages he hardly ever read, mostly in the Bible's New Testament. Now he tried to read them over and over to gain understanding.

Brent's dark mood was cheered by playing soccer amidst the smiling barrio street boys. Argentinean men never paid much attention to these ragged boys. Their fathers had disappeared into the labyrinth of the *villa miserias*, dealing drugs, doing drugs, and murdering rival gang members. Many were in jail. Mere boys became the heads of their houses, helping their mothers with the burden of feeding smaller children. When they could, they transformed into kids again, playing soccer in the dusty alley ways of the safer neighborhoods.

Naturally missing the company of men, the street boys looked up to Brent and Ammon, who played with them and demonstrated a few tricks with a ball and foot. Brent's *el Castellano* was so fluent he could talk to them about more than religion. *El Castellano* was Castilian Spanish, and Brent loved speaking it.

"We saw you dance a tango down by the railroad tracks," José teased.

"But your girlfriend was very skinny," said 10-year-old Emilio, giggling, "skinny as a broomstick."

Brent laughed. "Only because she *was* a broomstick. What were you doing? Spying on us? Don't you have anything better to do?"

"We should ask you the same thing," José said. "Why are you here? You bring us your religion, but we have our own religion. Yours is strange to us."

"I think you'd like it if you understood more," replied Ammon gently. "We could explain it all to you and your mama if you allow us."

"Mama says no, she does not trust outsiders."

"Okay, you guys," said Brent. "Enough about that. One reason we're here is to start a real soccer team with authentic shirts. Your families can come and watch you play."

"A real team? You would help us?" asked Emilio.

More street boys stepped up to hear their dreams come true.

"Who wants to join?" asked Brent. "Get all your friends together, and bring them back here. If we have enough boys for two teams, Elder Carr will coach one, and I'll coach the other. We'll practice for our first tournament starting tomorrow afternoon about four."

Brent knew he'd have to put out a little money and get some prizes sent from America, but it would be worth it if the Argentineans trusted them enough to accept the LDS gospel.

■　■　■

"It's a brilliant idea," said Ammon over their meager dinner in the small apartment on the safer outskirts of the slums. Brent mapped out for him the logistics of his plan.

"I like it too, mostly because I miss my younger brothers. These boys kind of remind me of them."

"I miss my family, too, only I have sisters."

"Anyway, as we coach, we can tell stories about heroes from the Book of Mormon. The parents might learn to like us and invite us into their homes." Brent tried to look confident.

"Right, and in three of four home visits, we'll have baptisms." Ammon pulled his Missionary Handbook out of his breast pocket.

"You're not going to find it in those rules," said Brent, "I already looked.

Soccer's not considered a contact sport, so we're allowed to play it, and besides, Elder Carr, we're only the coaches. This will generate baptisms, I guarantee it."

■   ■   ■

After practice the next day, the boys drifted back into the *villas miserias* to their homes. Brent and Ammon pushed their bicycles alongside them, making sure they got home safe. The neighborhood showed signs of gang activity with new graffiti and drug paraphernalia lying on the ground in plain sight.

Emilio, a tall boy of ten, had been chosen by the other boys to be captain of Brent's team. He pushed a rock on the ground with his foot, holding a new highly prized ball that Brent had purchased.

"I don't know this hero Nephi who is in your book," said Emilio, "but I know about the Pope in Rome, Pope Francisco from Argentina. Many people see him when he comes back."

Ammon's face formed a dark cloud, and Brent had to hide his own dismay at the mention of the much admired Pope.

"Pope Francisco cares about poor people," Emilio said. "He says God cares about us, too. My mother says he can change the world, the world that doesn't care about the poor."

"I hope you know we care about you," said Brent, "because we do." He felt keenly that it wasn't enough; they really didn't have much to offer these people of the slums.

Bang! Bang! In less than a second, the boys disappeared toward the sound, attracted like magnets to anything that drew them out of their mundane lives. Hoping it wasn't gunfire, Brent and Ammon jumped on their bikes and followed them down an alley. The gaggle of barrio boys bent their necks over a pipe railing built on a high cement retaining wall.

In the impossibly narrow road below, a rusty white van was stopped, still running. To his relief, Brent saw white smoke and realized this van had backfired. The vehicle was up against a ten-foot pile of garbage, which made the street into a dead end. Wafting through the area was the pungent odor of rotten food and human waste.

"They are lost! Lost!" the boys shouted. "*Americanos* in danger!"

How did the boys know Americans were inside? Then he spotted a crooked magnetic sign clinging to the door. In both English and Spanish it read *Faith Bible Church*. A lithe young woman with dark hair pulled back in a ponytail got out. Lifting sunglasses to the top of her head, she peered at the crowd at the railing where the boys and the missionaries stood gawking.

In perfect Spanish, she asked, "Does anyone know the way to the Christian orphanage?"

"We do, we'll show you!" Brent shouted in English, taking charge with a rush of adrenaline. He swung under the railing, perched atop the eight-foot wall, and jumped down, landing with deeply bent knees, like he had at home on the trampoline when he was a kid.

The young woman looked surprised to see a white-shirted Mormon missionary step up beside her. The group of pre-teen boys ran down the street to climb down at a lower place, although some daredevils copied Brent. Ammon got down somehow, appearing at Brent's side.

"This is Elder Carr, and I'm Elder Young. The boys here know this area, and it's a dangerous neighborhood. You're Americans?"

"You guessed it. I'm Rachel Christenson. Nice to meet you, but first it looks like I need to back out of here. There's no way to turn around." Her face twitched slightly.

A window rolled down, and another young woman stuck her head out. "Is it okay, Rachel?"

"Yes, Alison, these guys know where the orphanage is. We have room for you if you'd like to get inside." Rachel slid the side door open. A man and woman in the back climbed out. "This is Josh and his wife, Janie," Rachel said.

"We'll get our bikes and show you the way," Ammon said blandly, signaling with his expressive face to Brent. Riding with people they hardly knew was forbidden in the Handbook.

"It's too far, and trouble's coming," Brent told him. Ammon reneged to Brent's leadership with a shrug.

"Trouble?" asked Josh.

"This neighborhood's a violent one, and you're up against this barricade. That's just where the local gang wants their victims."

Rachel's smile faded. "Oh, oh. Let's get the bikes up top then."

"Better hurry," said Brent. They lifted the bikes up, and Josh stood on the floorboard of the van to secure them with bungee cords.

Every single boy had left the vicinity. Highly unusual, unless they knew someone was coming that way. "I'll drive," Brent said, taking over the driver's seat. "We've got to get out fast."

Rachel looked startled but climbed into the passenger seat. Ammon dove into the back with the two women and Josh. Just as the doors closed, a group of men in hoods entered the area from a shadowy side street. Brent slammed the van into reverse and floored the gas, turning his head all the way around to view the back window. Steering backwards in a narrow alley at full speed, his necktie choking him, he managed to find a place to turn around and escape the garbage-infested neighborhood.

No one said a word for a while.

Rachel spoke first. "You were *so* in the right place at the right time! These streets aren't exactly on our GPS."

"That had to be God," Josh added from the back. "Thanks, my wife's prayers were answered, right, honey?" She nodded.

"You two are our angels today. I'm Alison, by the way," said the girl with the auburn braid.

Brent loosened his tie into a loop around his perspiring neck. "We don't usually go into that area, do we, Elder Carr?"

"No, and after today, we'll be meeting the soccer boys somewhere else. That was close," Ammon said. "Turn here, Elder Young, and you'll avoid the open sewer. The orphanage is a few minutes from here, in a way safer area."

They drove into a brick cobbled square where a two-story stone building stood. In front of the orphanage, a group of panting boys waited for them, and surrounded the van like lapping tidewaters, chanting, "*Americanos, Americanos.*"

Brent shook his head in disbelief. "Looks like our soccer boys ran ahead to see if we'd make it out of there," he said, concentrating on driving slowly through the mass of kids.

Ammon said, "Yep, they're here at the finish line, to see if the *gringos* made it out of the barrio hole alive. Sure was exciting for them."

"A little too exciting for us, but we made it, thanks to you," Rachel said softly, with a sideways glance at Brent.

Maria, the director of the Faith in Jesus orphanage, stood like a taller and stouter plant growing amongst the lawn of boys, waving at the van. The adventure was over for now, and they all got out.

Spreading her arms in wide hugs for each of them, Maria welcomed the shaken new arrivals. "Welcome, friends from America." With surprise, she saw the two missionaries and hugged them, kissing the air close to their ears. "All my friends from America are here. I haven't seen you two for some time." She spoke English well, trilling the R's with a flourish. Most of the boys scattered after examining the van for bullet holes.

The group of young people assessed one another. Brent warmed to the idea that here were Americans who came to help the poor children in the slums of Buenos Aires, just as he and Ammon were doing.

"We're from Utah," he told them, helping them unload the crowded van. "Where are you all from?"

"Wow," said Josh, "we love Utah. We went to Moab on our honeymoon last year, didn't we, Janie? We're all from the same church in Portland, Oregon. We're on a short-term mission for our young adult group."

Brent noticed sweat soaking through Ammon's bright white shirt and wondered if he looked as damp as his companion. He loosened his daypack and felt his wet back under it. In Argentina, summer began in December. Even November could be hot. It was probably 80 degrees today.

They unloaded mountains of supplies from inside the van. Brent saw that these American girls shone even in the stench of the barrio, without makeup, yet clear and alive with enthusiasm, their loveliness coming from within. They exuded confidence now that they were at the orphanage and Rachel regained her poise.

"You don't know how much you're needed here," he said, trying to encourage them. "We can't give much time to help, but we did put up the water system."

Maria pointed to the barrels on the rooftop. "Look what these two did for us. Now we have good warm water."

"You guys got those 55-gallon drums up on the roof yourselves?" Josh asked.

Brent and Ammon looked down while Maria nodded briskly. "They are sweet boys, those two, with good hearts."

Ammon said, "Maria fights for these malnourished kids. They need clothes, too. Elder Young and I have tried, but we can't do much, so we're glad you came." Ammon was the most compassionate guy Brent knew.

"That's what all these boxes are for," said Josh. "Medicine, food and clothes."

Brent knew Maria had prayed long and hard for all these items. He'd overheard her once, in the stairwell, asking God for supplies. "Jesus be praised," Maria said, clapping her hands together. "I did not know you bring so much."

Alison stepped up. "We'll be here for three months and have access to even more. So if you find we can help other children in the barrio, let us know, Elders."

Brent looked at his watch. "We have to go, Senora Maria, but we'll be back next week, to help the reinforcements."

Rachel smiled right at him when he said it.

Walking over to him, she said in a low tone, "You got us out of a tight place back there. I'm such a dolt for getting our team lost like that. Anything could've happened. Thanks again for saving us, Elder Young. That was God's love in action." Her eyes beamed warmth. Talking more with this American girl was all Brent could think about. He knew he shouldn't, but he couldn't help it.

Brent thought about her as they rode their bikes to the middle-class area where their apartment was. His trained mind had been taught to constantly highlight the LDS Church, to do what it taught, to show how exceptional LDS doctrines were and to defend them. He was trained to convince people that the Latter Day Saints had absolute truth, far above any other religion. These Bible Christians, on the other hand, barely mentioned any church but they sure talked about Jesus and God's love all the time.

Ammon must've been thinking about something else. "Hey, how about that Alison?" he asked, with his characteristic understated grin.

Brent relaxed. "Yeah, Rachel's cool, too." He was happier than he had been for a while during the long, unproductive year. "They're about our age, don't you think?"

"Yeah, twenty, maybe. Enough said." Ammon laughed. "We're going to go back to help. Rules still apply, though. I won't let you out of my sight, Elder Young."

Chapter Sixteen
Moving the Wasatch

Alex awoke on a December morning hoping he and Jennalee were meant for each other after all. Since Pastor Ron and his wife dated while *she* was a Mormon, it was possible to have a happy outcome. But working more hours kept him from spending time with Jennalee. The next day, he finally had a Saturday off of work, so they planned to go to Wolf Mountain Ski Resort.

He dropped Gabe off at junior high as it started to snow, and got to his locker almost late for his first class. His confidence waned today, especially when he saw Cory loitering near Jennalee's locker. Conversing with Jennalee would be impossible with Cory hanging around. He zigzagged across the hall to get a closer look, hoping to get her to walk with him halfway to class as was their habit.

It looked like Jennalee was flirtatious that morning . . . with Cory. Why was she acting like that? Alex was crushed, his confidence bottoming at a real low. Never in his life had feelings for a girl been like this: soaring one minute and diving the next.

"So when's your boyfriend coming to Seminary?" Cory asked, his back to Alex.

"What?" asked Jennalee.

"That Alex guy, when's he going to get with the program and join the Church?"

"Go away, Cory," she said as Alex walked up behind him. He felt anger rise like a tsunami and tapped Cory on the shoulder. When he spun around, Alex closed in, inches away from the guy's shocked face.

"Did you hear her? She said go away. What don't you understand about that?"

Alex sensed students stop and wait for the impending fight.

"Alex . . ." Jennalee darted between them.

"That's what you said, isn't it, Jennalee? For him to go away?"

"Cory, you better go now," she said, in a practiced calm way.

Cory slunk down the hall. Alex thought if the guy had a tail, it would've been between his legs.

Now Jennalee got in *his* face. "Totally uncalled for, Alex," she said, almost hissing like a cat. Striding towards the mob of kids waiting for some action, she announced, "Okay, it's all over now."

He waited for the crowd to disperse, then said in a low voice, "He's jealous, that's why he's harassing you."

"Maybe. But you are, too. Why, Alex?"

Alex was dizzy and hot, at a loss for words to describe how his angst. How did he let himself be drawn in by a girl who'd grown up LDS? Could he ever be a true part of her life?

"I'm sorry, I lost it." He hung his head. "My fault. I heard him say stuff about me."

"Cory gets carried away sometimes. Don't take it personally, Alex. I have five brothers, so I'm used to being hassled. Anyway, what he said was more against me than you."

"If it's against you, then I do take it personally. Usually I don't get so mad, but you acted like you liked him."

She exhaled. "I've known him since I was three, okay? Really, I don't like him in the way you're thinking. I'm sorry, too." Her tone reassured him. "I care way more about you, Alex. I have a game to cheer after school today, but we're still going skiing tomorrow, right? Pick me up early, okay?"

"Yeah, okay." His worries clung so hard to his chest he couldn't breathe.

■　■　■

Saturday morning, five inches of fresh snow, and her skis thrown in the back of his truck, they headed up the mountain, heater blasting. Jennalee owned the latest skis and boots, but Alex had to rent gear when they got to the lodge. She looked pretty as always in a sky blue sweater that offset her eyes.

Alex was on top of the world with her beside him.

"I bet you're happy to have a day off," she said. "I've been traveling so much with cheerleading and you've been working, so I miss our times together. Why'd you want to come here, though, when you work at Powder Mountain?"

"A friend gave me a two-for-one ticket, and I don't like seeing any of the regulars up at Powder."

Earlier that month, they'd agreed to read each other's Scriptures, but Alex found he didn't like the Book of Mormon. He knew how much this would hurt her. The trouble was, the King James language it used was archaic, and he disliked reading it. Most people he knew preferred to read the ESV or NIV versions of the Bible to escape the 'Thees' and 'Thous' in the King James. The Book of Mormon had no easier translations; it was what it was.

The Bible clearly said that Jesus' work was finished and handed it all over to his disciples when he ascended into heaven. His disciples spread the gospel around the world. So why would Jesus come to the New World and appear to Nephites and Lamanites? Alex couldn't keep it all straight. Jesus' disciples were his hands and feet on the earth, and Alex himself was one of them, sent to Utah.

"So did you read the book of Nephi?" Jennalee finally asked. The air in the truck cab became tense.

"Yes, and it's confusing to me. So have you read the Gospel of John yet?"

"You think you're confused? So am I," she countered, as if she knew what he was thinking about the Book of Mormon.

Patience, he told himself. He reached for the New Testament he kept in the truck door cubby and tossed it on her lap as he drove.

"Read me the first part of John. It starts with Matthew, Mark, Luke, and then John. Show me what you don't understand."

"Okay, here it is: 'In the beginning was the Word, and Word was with

God, and the Word was God. He was with God in the beginning. Through Him all thing were made; without Him nothing was made that has been made. In Him was life, and that life was the light of all mankind.'"

Alex said, "John means that the Word is Jesus."

"That means Jesus is God and created all things."

"Right. John says Jesus is and was eternal, that He is God, and was with God and then He was the Light who came to earth. At Christmas, the Light was born."

"This is new," Jennalee said, "I was taught that Jesus is our brother, born from Heavenly Father and Heavenly Mother exactly like you and me. Then he came to earth."

"Heavenly Mother? Wait a minute, are you saying they have sex in heaven?" He blinked hard a few times.

"That's the way people are created, Alex," she retorted in a snide voice.

Alex mustered mercy and said, "Only we're not talking about people here. We're talking about God the Father and Jesus His Son. Jennalee, you have to read it for what it says. You can't put the beliefs you were taught into it. The Bible is as it is written and it tells the truth. It says Jesus is God."

"That's what you were taught. And he is, but not like you think, Alex."

He stepped on the gas pedal and sped up on a straightaway. "The Bible is the Word of God, not man's theology or what I was taught. How do you understand it then?"

"Jesus isn't the same as Heavenly Father. They're two different personages."

"That's so strange to me. Jenn, if you read the Bible without those ideas, and pray for understanding, you'll get it. Dismantle the religious stuff and read what the words really say." Everything he'd talked about with Pastor Ron went out the window as he steered on to the snow-covered road to Wolf Mountain.

"It's the same with the Book of Mormon, Alex. I'm almost afraid to ask what you really think of it." She took a deep breath. He could see how serious she was.

"And I'm almost afraid to tell you," he said, "but here it is. It's like reading Shakespeare, which is in the same old English." He couldn't say how their book annoyed him with pretentious words and the repetitions of, "And it came to pass."

He sensed a cloud passing over the sky of her bright face. "The words are translated exactly from Heavenly Father to the Prophet Joseph Smith from golden plates. Your Bible in its many translations is incorrect, but our Book of Mormon is the most correct book on earth."

"Jennalee, let's not argue. I've heard this before, what you believe about the Bible. Why do you carry it as part of your sacred Scriptures, but don't believe what it says?"

She parried. "We respect the Bible as far as it is translated correctly; but it's not our main Scripture. The Book of Mormon is." She folded her arms with a pouty attitude.

"Okay, I'll keep reading Nephi if you read the rest of the John. But let me tell you: the Bible *is* reliable. It's God's Word and He wouldn't let it be corrupted. You've been told different, but the Bible is true. Every word of it."

"I'll try to understand it, I really will, Alex."

"Don't read any ideas into it. Just what it says, like a child reading it for the first time, okay?"

"Okay," she agreed as he parked his light pickup in the snowy parking lot. "Let's forget this discussion and go have some fun."

"You're right. We can talk about it later, no hard feelings." After opening the door for her, he strode up to the kiosk to pay for the lift.

Jennalee skipped to keep up with him. "Who gave you the two-for-one? Tony?"

"Actually, it was Madeline," he told her. "So now I can afford more than hot dogs for lunch." He laughed, not wanting to tell her that the original idea a few months ago was for him to bring Madeline herself.

Jennalee took his hand. "Madeline must be a good friend."

"Just that, a friend. She may be here today, she told me."

"Nice. Here's the rental hut," said Jennalee. "I'll run to the rest room to put my stuff on."

Minutes later, when Alex came out with his gear, he noticed the fitted lavender down jacket and matching snow pants made her look pretty indeed.

She wasn't afraid to be feminine like some girls. And next to her, chatting away, was Madeline.

"Hey, thanks for the tickets, helps a lot." Alex couldn't help but notice that Madeline, too, looked perfect in an on-the-slopes rose-colored parka, her dark hair in a high pony tail.

"About time you made it here," Madeline said, "and you, too, Jennalee. How about that quiz on Friday? I bet I missed every question."

They talked about Chemistry class for a few minutes as Madeline kept her eyes on the slope of downhill skiers.

"Looking for someone?" asked Jennalee.

"I see him." She waved. "Here he comes." Five seconds later, a lanky young man in gray came to a stop next to her in a swoosh of snow.

"Show-off," Madeline said. "This is my friend Roy."

They exchanged names. Roy, a tall African-American with close-cropped hair, took off his gloves and shook hands with them, tucking his goggles on his head.

"How about this new powder? I'm not too good at skiing or I'd be on those moguls. Basketball is my sport. I play varsity for Layton Christian." Roy put his arm around Madeline playfully.

"Your coach let you go skiing?" Alex asked. "If I was good enough to play varsity, I'd save my legs."

"Shh," Roy said, "my coach doesn't know I'm here, and Madeline got us great tickets."

"Us, too. Madeline's the one to know. Let's meet up for lunch. We should be able to get in four runs and meet here at noon."

The fresh powder burned his face as he sped down the mountain, following the lavender lady, who zoomed far ahead. He had a hard time keeping up with a Utah native. When he caught up, they skied tandem down to the lodge, snow flying in their faces. He wished fervently for the same togetherness in faith, because he was falling hard for Jennalee.

From then on, the day was perfect. Madeline and Roy were fun to hang with, and on the way home, they avoided the entire subject of religion and talked about their dreams for the future. After the skirmish of the morning, religion was once again a topic to be lightly touched, as though with the feathers of an angel's wing, but he knew it would come up again.

The only answer was that one of them would have to change faiths. He had to admit that hers had a lot to offer, even if he could see doctrinal issues. His other choice would be incredibly hard. He didn't think he'd be able to extricate himself from the relationship. He didn't want to; it wasn't fair that he should have to. Maybe they'd work it out.

Chapter Seventeen
The Crossroads

What a relationship it was, both of them padding softly, not mentioning the spiritual mountains standing like a barrier between them. Alex so often wanted to take her into his arms and pretend she was his, and that she'd always be there, but he knew their feet were mired down in positions miles away from each other.

The only answer was either to ignore religion or agree to be in the same one. It was all so jumbled in Alex's brain. He'd have to convince her to change because he realized at this point he could not become a Latter-day Saint. It was now unthinkable, not because of abstention from coffee or dressing up in a suit for church every Sunday, but because he knew, in his heart of hearts, that something in the doctrines of the LDS Church was wrong. He couldn't easily prove it, and he couldn't convince Jennalee without proof.

As though their relationship would go on forever, they paid no attention to the looming date of graduation in May, five months away. And because his part-time jobs stood in the way of seeing her, he constantly thought she'd find someone else. Sure, they talked and texted. Now with her previous boyfriend Bridger back from his Mission, Alex's paranoia grew, and he'd text her all the more.

Time edged to Christmas Day, the second one with Dad in heaven.

One afternoon shortly before Christmas he picked Gabe up from school and drove west, looking into the sunset. They ended up on the seven-mile causeway leading to Antelope Island, in the middle of the Great Salt Lake. The salt water went on for miles on either side of it, the wind causing foamy white waves. It was a wild spot, exposed to the elements from every side.

Alex had homework, his job at the coffee house, and chores at home, but he kept driving on and on, needing to escape those pressures. He could tell Gabe enjoyed the company, even though his brother was quiet.

"Look at all that salt water. It doesn't have fish in it, does it?" Gabe asked.

"The only life in it are brine shrimp and brine flies. Sea monkeys, remember those? Oh, and the seagulls."

"That's the state bird," Gabe said, "because during pioneer days, a plague of crickets ate the crops. Seagulls came and ate the crickets and saved the harvest."

"Hm. Interesting story. Spiritually speaking, though, this lake is symbolic, Gabe. We're in a dry and thirsty land with no living water to drink. This island is about the loneliest, most God-forsaken place on the planet."

"Yeah, I know, I mean, look at it!" Gabe pointed to the Great Salt Lake. "All that water, and not a drop to drink."

"Yeah, and back in town, there's a church every four blocks. The place is full of religion, but what about actual relationships with Jesus? It's so uncomfortable here because we're not in their group. Not that I want to be."

"You should know, Alex. You've been finding out about Mormonism with Jennalee."

"I found out I don't much like the religion, but I sure like the girl. At the same time, I miss home. Do you? I miss our friends and visiting Dad's grave."

"I know, huh? Can we drive back to Oregon for Christmas break?"

Alex sighed. "I have two jobs and work at the ski resort the whole time. It's their big moneymaking season."

"And then there's your girlfriend. Guess we can't forget her. Or Mom and Carl." Gabe was quiet. "What do you think of Carl, Alex?"

"He's a nice guy, but I don't want Mom to marry him. He's too old. And it's too soon after Dad died."

"It's okay for you," said Gabe, "you don't have five years of school left. I don't want a stepdad yet."

"I see your point. I'd be gone, and you wouldn't. I don't think Mom wants to marry him, Gabe, but if she does, I can take you to Italy with me. You know enough of the language to go to school there. Nonna would feed you pasta until you were a big tubby boy."

It was good to hear Gabe laugh. "Thanks a lot. Seriously, that's not a bad idea. Utah is like a foreign country and at least I'm familiar with Italy. Are you really thinking of taking the job for Uncle Lucio?"

"Yep. Oh, whoa." Alex stopped the truck. "There's a buffalo herd coming this way!"

Missing them by inches, the big animals stampeded past. Alex snapped pictures with his phone, and took a selfie of the two of them, open-mouthed at the hairy beasts. Dust settled on the truck and sifted through on to their hair.

"They're not really wild, they're tame," Gabe said. "They feed them back there at that corral, so they're running like a bunch of sheep." Wind swirled eddies of grass and dirt around the truck, striking the glass with small pebbles.

"Right, they're more like zoo animals, running for food every day at the same time. Reminds me of people, going to the same trough to be fed day in and day out." Would his brother catch his sarcasm?

"So it's not like the Wild West after all," agreed Gabe. "They don't know how to live by their own efforts anymore."

"Remember this, Gabe, we have to think for ourselves to be free. That's it, I'm going to Italy for sure to learn the wine business."

"Can I go, too? I hated the year we skipped Italy, because Dad died. I wish we'd moved there."

"Me, too, bro. But even if I'm there, and you're here with Mom, we can Facetime. Unless Mom marries Carl. Then you can come with me for sure."

■   ■   ■

On the phone, Jennalee insisted they go downtown on his next day off. He worked double shifts on weekends, so on a Tuesday, the week before Christmas, they planned to go. "We can ice skate at the Salt Palace, go out to eat, and then over to see the Christmas lights at Temple Square. It's a tradition here."

He had to find her a Christmas present. So the day before, after his job at Starbucks, he'd driven to the only Christian Bookstore in Salt Lake City. He wanted to make the occasion something special.

The sun had long set when Alex picked up Jennalee. She wore skinny jeans and a long sweater coat, mittens, and a hat. She was so pretty, riding next to him as they headed downtown. His mind went back to the swirl of things Pastor Ron had told him. And after church on Sunday, a guy about his Dad's age, Jeff Allred, had taken Alex out for breakfast. He told him about his previous life in the Mormon faith and opened Alex up to the differences between his world and Jennalee's world. There were many.

But here she was, excited to be with him, and he with her. They found parking near the Salt Palace. It took all he could do to keep up with Jennalee on the rink. The last time he fell, he said, "Okay, okay. You win. You're an awesome skater, Jenn."

They took their skates off and exchanged them for their shoes at the kiosk. Chilly air blew around them like the inside of a fridge, and he suggested warming up and getting a bite to eat somewhere before they strolled to the temple grounds. Alex wanted the perfect place to give her his gift.

She looked up at him with her blue eyes sparkling under the streetlights. "First let's go to the temple and see the lights," she said. "We'll warm up as we walk. Every year the displays get more spectacular, and sometimes the Tab choir sings carols. C'mon." She took his hand and started leading him up North Temple Street to Temple Square.

"Tab Choir?" he repeated.

"The Mormon Tabernacle Choir, silly. I know you've heard of them."

"Right. You sure you don't want something to eat first?" He held her gloved hand and got into stride, trying to forget about going into one of the warm cafés they passed.

"Not now. After we look around we'll go to Lion House Pantry Restaurant." She giggled. "You know, the house with all the little windows?"

"How can I forget? Hey, I'm putty in your hands. Not only are you one of the best ice skaters I know, you're really strong." He dusted the crusty frost from his knees. Every time he'd fallen, Jennalee stood tall over him, offering a helping hand. She kept her balance every time.

"You weren't that bad," she said. "What was it? Your third time skating?"

"Right, only it's embarrassing, because you're so good."

"Here we are," she announced, "all streets lead to Temple Square."

"So it appears," he said, with uneasiness, "but the gates to the temple are closed, at least they are for me."

"The lights are all outside. Alex Campanaro, I'm surprised at you. We don't leave anybody out if they believe."

He wished things were so simple. He was a believer all right, but not in what she believed.

"Alex, isn't it the most beautiful place in the world, all lit up like that?" She stood and stared at the grand temple shooting spires up from the landscaped square. Other couples milled around gazing at tiny clusters of lights climbing each tree and netted over bushes. Smiling strangers volunteered to take pictures of them.

He tried to enjoy it all, but was overcome with apprehension at the ghostly greenish lights shining on the temple. He'd thought it would be romantic, standing there with Jennalee. He should kiss her, to make the moment special, but found he couldn't, not here in the shadow of the temple. In his soul, Alex knew it was more than a building that stood between them. He glanced at the reflecting pool near the Tabernacle where sounds of the famous choir rang out from the domed building. The Christmas carols only fogged his brain further.

It struck him that under these stunning lights, he could give her his gift. That would be romantic, the way he wanted this night to be.

"I have something for you," he said, biting his lip in the cold, "I got you a Christmas gift."

Jennalee put her hands on her hips, her white sweater coat reflecting the colored lights. "Oh, Alex, thank you. I have one for you, too, but I accidentally left it at home."

"I hope you like it." He slipped the little box out of his pocket and onto her snow white glove. Kissing her cheek, he whispered, "Merry Christmas."

She put her chin up and looked directly into his eyes. "You can kiss me better than that."

"Open it first," Alex said, his heart strangely pounding. It looked like a ring box in her hand, and he wondered if she might mistake it for one. She might think it was a promise ring and be disappointed.

"Wonder what you bought for me?" she said, untying the red bow around the box, her cheeks pink in the cold.

"I hope you like it," he said, suddenly unsure of himself. He glanced at the spires of the temple in the night sky, glowing as though coated with effervescent paint.

"Alex, what are you staring at?"

"I can't see a cross on the temple. Maybe it's too dark."

"There aren't crosses on it." She looked at him quizzically and opened the box. Her expression changed from delight to shock. She lifted the necklace and Alex saw the glimmer of the tiny silver cross. He felt heavy inside.

"Oh, Alex."

"You don't like it, do you?" His hope shattered like a fallen icicle.

"I need to explain to you what we believe. Let's go warm up at the bakery."

She clasped his hand in hers again, and they walked in silence out the gates and round the corner to the little restaurant at the back of her great-grandfather's Lion House. They sat at a table and she ordered the famous hot chocolate. He bought the same because there was no coffee, though he needed the shot of energy it gave him. She put the boxed necklace on the table.

"I'm sorry, Alex, we don't wear crosses. We think it's a symbol of murder, similar to wearing a guillotine. It's not something we use in our religion."

Alex swallowed hard. "I'm the one who's sorry, Jenn. I should have noticed that there aren't any on your church steeples and none on the temple. I never saw a cross in a cemetery in Utah, either. Why does your Church disregard the Cross?"

"It's not that, Alex. It isn't that important to us; it's not sacred to us. Personally, I think we should use it more."

"Now you've reached the crux of the matter." He could see she didn't catch the Latin word. "Let me get this right. The Church of Jesus Christ of the Latter-day Saints doesn't acknowledge the full redemption of the Cross of Jesus Christ, where he gave his life to save us. Yet LDS claim they are

Christians." He could hear the outrage in his voice; he didn't want to be angry, he just was.

"You make us sound like we're not Christian, and we are." Her face twisted with some indignation of her own.

He willed himself to calm down. "Jenn, Christ-followers wear crosses to remember Jesus' sacrifice, to say to the world that we are his and he is ours. It's a symbol of the only way humankind can be saved."

"We don't think of it that way," she said, sounding defensive. "The Church teaches the Atonement came at the Garden of Gethsemane."

The hair on the back of his neck went up and Alex jerked to attention. "Gethsemane? That's new to me."

"Our Savior shed drops of blood there. The Atonement at Gethsemane saved us." Her voice quavered. "It's what I've been taught, Alex."

He could hardly inhale in the stifling atmosphere of the restaurant. "I believe the Atonement happened at the Cross on Calvary, the second Jesus died when he took on the sin of the world. The sky was darkened. The earth shook. And the veil at the Jewish Temple keeping all of us from approaching God without a high priest? It was torn in two at that very moment."

She sniffed. "I don't think we can agree on this."

He held his hand up. "Gethsemane doesn't make sense to me as the place where the Atonement happened." His thoughts spun, and it underlined what Jeff Allred had said about how deep the differences in their beliefs were. Realization dawned on him that Tony's warnings about going out with a Mormon may have been right. Were his beliefs as surprising to her as hers were to him? At this moment she seemed like an alien who would never understand him, and more importantly, she couldn't understand the truth written about Jesus.

She regarded him with knitted brows as he stewed. "Please, Alex, I'll keep the cross, but I can't wear it. You didn't know, and it's a good gift from your heart. I'm sorry you're upset." He saw she was trying not to cry.

He sighed long and deep. The cross on the table in its box emblazoned the space between them like a wall of fire, but courage surged in his soul. "Keep it, Jenn, in memory of someone who loves you. I'll take you home now. We can talk more about it later."

■   ■   ■

Alone in his room that night, he punched his pillow in anger. The romance of the Temple lights and the perfect date was forever turned sour by the mire of religion. Memories of his dad's bedroom, the room he died in, resurfaced in his mind. Alex spent countless hours there just being with him, loving him. On the wall opposite the borrowed hospice bed hung a cross. Dad had slipped out of this world gazing at that cross, fully understanding the meaning behind it. That cross was the last thing his father saw before Jesus ushered him to heaven. Alex pounded his pillow again.

He wasn't only hurt at how Jennalee spurned his gift; he was utterly confused. For the first time since meeting her, he could see differences large enough to split them up. In his torn thoughts, he knew one thing. Never could he take the true Cross of Christ out of his life. It ran as deep as his DNA.

Is this how evangelists felt in a dark place with pagans who had no true knowledge of God? But Mormons weren't pagan, they were religious. There had to be a right place to stand in all of this. Getting on his knees against his bed, he prayed, "Lord God, I want to follow you with all my heart, my soul, and my might. Help me, I don't know what to say to Jennalee. I'm in a dry and weary place where there's no Living Water. What should I do? Can you show her how much you love her? Help her to know you in a way she understands. Not my will, but yours be done." The wall of his room echoed back his words, and he felt totally alone.

Chapter Eighteen
Mountains Moved

All of Christmas vacation Alex spent looking at the backsides of skiers catching his chair lift and riding up the mountain. As lift operator at Powder Mountain, at least he had ample time to think. He ruminated and fretted, and all because of that gorgeous Mormon girl. Did he love her?

He was at a crisis, sitting on a stool at a lonely job in the cold. People paid him only the attention they'd give a tree stump. After this job, he resolved to be kinder to service people working in lowly positions.

The money earned here was earmarked for Italy. Once he got there, his family would help him achieve success. He told himself that sometimes you had to start at the bottom. Literally, he thought wryly, watching people plop themselves on to the moving chairs.

Alex decided to investigate more about the origins of the LDS religion, and with the little time he had between jobs, he drove to the South Ogden library. A whole shelf in the Dewey 200s was marked with an *M* for Mormon. Most of these books were Mormon apologetics and history written by the fathers of the Church. That wasn't what he was looking for.

He'd hunt for the truth and not give up. The sheer numbers of books on the Prophet Joseph Smith in this Utah library amazed him. As many as priests in Rome. Sitting on the floor with a curious title called *No Man Knows My History*, he began to read. If he was madly in love with Brigham Young's great-granddaughter, then he'd better look into this history. Even if no man knew it, he'd find out what really happened at the start of the Mormon religion. He began reading in the library till they closed, then at home, only putting it down at midnight.

Jennalee made lame excuses not to see him during Winter break. They weren't together the entire time, only texting once in a while. Sure enough, the wall had become higher, the wall between faiths.

They were barely in touch, but he wanted to reach out to her as soon as his job let up. He honestly didn't want to lose her. Then, on New Year's Day, she showed up near his chair lift, where she took off her skis and punched them into a snow drift. He could tell she was happy to see him, but he hesitated to show how glad he was to see her. She talked to him as he worked.

"My whole family's here," she said, her breath frosty, "so I thought I'd come by and say 'hi'. You work too much; it's really hard to get together, Alex."

"And you play too much," he replied, not meaning to sound so bitter.

She ignored his jibe and went on in an excited voice. "Alex, you know those horses in parades with black ovals over their eyes so they look straight ahead and won't see anything else?"

What random thing was she talking about? Miserable from constant early morning risings and late nights, Alex answered robotically, "Yeah, I know what you mean."

"I was like one of those horses. See, my life slowed down over the break, and I read the entire Book of John in a modern version of the Bible that made it alive to me. I'm like a new person without those blinders. I can see a wider picture now."

Alex stood suddenly and his stool fell over in the snow. "You read the whole thing, Jenn?" Long curls escaped as he adjusted his beanie hat. "I'm so glad, but I wish I didn't have to work because I can't talk about it right now," he said, barely managing to adjust a lever on the lift in time. "I can't dump anyone or I get fired."

"What time do you get off for lunch?"

Here he was, the grungy, disheveled liftman, Alexander Dante Campanaro, talking to a lilac queen, Jennalee Eliza Young. People still ignored him.

"Lunch is at noon." His voice was hoarse. "They only give me half an hour, so can you get me some chili fries ahead of time? Then we can have the whole 30 minutes. I'll pay you back."

"I'll meet you in an hour with chili fries, I promise. I'll get you coffee, too. You look like you need it." She snapped her skis on and got in line.

Her brother Boston skied up beside her. "Where were you?" he asked, not noticing the liftman. Alex had to smile.

■   ■   ■

How feelings could soar when events changed! Hadn't he asked God to show her His love? So while he'd sat on his stool in the snow, full of self-pity, watching others have fun, the Holy Spirit of grace worked overtime. His prayer hadn't bounced off of his bedroom wall after all. It had reached heaven, and God shouldered the burden of every detail about her, about him, about their relationship. Only God could move mountains when they needed to be moved.

Jennalee had dropped long-awaited, hard-won news into his lap after two weeks of loneliness. This moment was crucial to their entire future. He rushed to the lodge at noon, where chili fries and a hot cup of coffee sat in the middle of a crowded table. Jennalee beamed at him, prettier than ever.

"Tell me more," he said, sitting on the picnic table's bench.

"Alex, you were right. If I read it without any learned ideas, like it's the first time, it gets clearer." She spoke in a low whisper, not only because her parents and brothers were eating a few feet away in another area, but because there were strangers at their picnic-style table. Her brothers waved at him and asked how he was doing, and he felt ecstatic and strange at the same time, wearing his liftman fluorescent vest like a shell on his back. With a cold look, her dad nodded his head at him, and got up to leave.

When he was gone, Alex touched her hand, forgetting the angst of the last two weeks. "You don't know how happy I am, Jenn."

"I feel different about the Bible now, Alex, I can't explain it, but I trust it more."

"I have to work the rest of the day. My first day off is the Sunday before school. Can we meet?" As he said it, he knew Sunday would be a problem for her.

She squeezed his hand. "It's the Sabbath and I can't, but let's meet at McDonald's Monday, like we used to. Then we can really talk."

■　■　■

It was like old times—he with his fast-food coffee, and her with a smoothie and an order of scrambled eggs. Yet it was different, because ever since she'd talked to him at Powder Mountain, Alex had been praying about this meeting.

"I take it you're caught up in AP Chemistry," he said.

She giggled. "I'm not taking that class this semester, now that I know you. It took my GPA down a notch, but it was worth it." Her eyes, brilliant blue in the morning sun, were untroubled, more open.

"So you got into AP Chem just to meet me?"

"Surely you knew."

He had suspected it. She got a book out of her backpack and put it in front of him. "Don't tell anyone, but I found this modern language version of the Bible and I really understand it. I felt guilty reading it but once I started I couldn't stop."

"I like it, too," he said, impressed. "It's a great start, Jenn. You don't know how glad I am. You really get it? You understand what the Book of John is saying?"

"I don't understand all of it, but in it, Jesus is different than I thought. I'm learning to follow what he says, not what everyone else says. I still have questions, but something happened to me while reading it, something I don't know how to describe in words, like my eyes opened."

His prayer for Jennalee to know the biblical Jesus was happening. "What if you talked to my pastor? He'd answer your questions. Did I tell you his wife used to be Mormon? They even dated while she was one, like us."

Jennalee looked puzzled. "Maybe I will talk to him, because I'm afraid of all these new thoughts."

"If I can explain anything, I'll try, Jennalee, but I think you should see

Pastor Ron, and after that, both of us should talk to him together."

"Okay, I'll have to sneak, though," she said, "because I'm in trouble if anyone finds out. My future is in jeopardy as it is."

"Your old planned-out future may change anyway, Jennalee. Here's Pastor's number. Feel free to text him and go to his house. I'm over there a lot. Well, me and Tony."

■　　■　　■

Days later, after her family had all gone to bed, Jennalee let herself out the side door of her garage. She started her car, which she'd parked on the street, and drove to Pastor Ron's. Checking for nosy neighbors, she saw only the flicker of televisions from darkened homes. It was a Thursday night, and she marveled at how exciting it was to be out so late.

So many questions! Her mind wavered with nagging doubts about going to a Protestant pastor instead of her bishop. But she'd already tried that route. After Alex had given her the cross, she'd seen the bishop of her ward, who told her to shelve her questions for a while and work harder to pray and believe. It was an answer that didn't satisfy, especially now that her thirst was whetted by reading the Book of John. She needed answers from someone outside of Mormonism.

What religious category was Pastor Ron in? Evangelical Protestant? His church was classified as Nondenominational on their website, saying they taught Biblical truth. Nervous twinges whirled in her stomach as soon as she drove up to the house.

Alex was close to this pastor, so Jennalee thought she could trust him. She wanted to find out about his church, her own, and the whole gamut of why there were so many churches in the first place. Joseph Smith said they were all wrong and that was why the Church of Jesus Christ of Latter-day Saints had to be established by God as the only correct one. But how could all the other churches be totally wrong? If truth was to be found, she wanted to find it. But it would take some courage.

Jennalee walked up the steps and knocked on the door of the simple old house. Plastic toys were scattered in the crumbling driveway, a tiny tricycle parked under a bush. Pastor Ron texted that his children would be in bed, so she knocked softly once more.

Turning to face the road, she noticed a curtain move inside a lit window across the street, making her even more nervous. Someone was watching. She wondered if the pastor knew his neighbors kept track of what went on in the neighborhood and, particularly, at his house.

Gulping cold air and longing for her warm bed, she wished she'd never dared to come. She pulled back to go home just as the door opened and a serene blond woman looked warmly at her.

"Welcome, Ms. Young! My husband said you'd be coming. Please come in. I'm Shannon."

"Hello," Jennalee said in a somber voice. "I know it's late, but this was the only time I could come."

"Absolutely okay," Shannon replied, "no worries. We're ready for guests any time around here. 'Instant in season and out of season,' as Paul told Timothy."

Her husband came into the room with a tray of steaming mugs. "Hot chocolate. Want some?"

After a little chitchat, Jennalee talked about the things nagging her ever since she'd met Alex Campanaro.

"Let me be clear. I'm LDS and my fourth great-grandfather was Brigham Young. I'm not the first of my clan to question the faith, but I'm here without my parents' knowledge. They wouldn't approve. I'm going out with Alex Campanaro, as you know. They don't approve of that, either."

The kind strangers didn't blink an eye. Nodding slightly, they seemed to understand her and just listened. Jennalee took a drink from her mug as if to sip courage. "I've been reading the Book of John. It makes me restless, and for the first time in my life, I don't believe every single thing my Church teaches. For instance, I know you must hear from God, too."

Pastor Ron laughed. "I hope I do," he said. "I pray to teach the Living Word of God as I hear it directly from Him, not from myself."

She paused. "I'm mainly here because I think I'm in love with Alex, and he says he loves me, too. We want to stay together, maybe marry."

Pastor Ron's voice was gentle. "You do have a lot of things to consider, Jennalee. How will your family react if you tell them you want to eventually marry Alex?"

"I have a lot to lose." Her throat tightened. "My family, my religion, a temple wedding. Alex says he has a lot at stake, too, but I have more. If I marry outside the Church, it would kill my mom and dad. I can barely think of it."

"What does Alex risk, do you think?"

"I know his mom doesn't want him to marry a Mormon, but she won't disown him even if she's mad."

The pastor nodded. "That's where you're not seeing the full picture, Jennalee."

"I'm not?"

"As you grow in Jesus, He'll show you more. Give yourself time to read even more of His Word."

"I'll try. See, I thought things would work out my way, the old way I'm comfortable with. I'm not ready to upset my parents and cause dissension in my family. But lately I started seeing ideas in the Bible that I could never understand before, and it's changing me."

"What you have to decide," said Shannon, "is whether to continue to grow and change in Christ or double back to your comfortable religion."

"Right, so why can't I stay Mormon and get to know Jesus, too?"

"That's a good question, Jennalee, and the answer is a personal one, directly from God and what He calls you to," Pastor Ron said.

He glanced at his wife, who affirmed him with a slight nod. "I'll tell you the truth, Jennalee. I'm here to point people to the Kingdom of God and help them see truth. It's available to all, but no one on this earth can see it without becoming born-again."

"I hear about being 'born-again' but it doesn't totally make sense. I know I was a Spirit Child in Heaven and I chose my earthly parents and my life, and was born on earth. Is that what you're talking about? The Pre-Existence?"

"Jennalee," Pastor Ron said in a soft tone, "that's LDS theology. God's Word is what I'm telling you. Listen, unless a person submits their will completely to the Creator, it's not possible to enter God's Kingdom. When you see a baby, it's a body you can hold, but the person who is shaped inside that little body is spirit. That spirit needs to be spiritually reborn to see God's true Kingdom." He paused. "It's absolutely real. The wind blows wherever it wants, and you can't see where it's coming from. God controls it. That's how it is with his Spirit when you completely submit your will to him. It's how you are born-again. Surrender to Him and trust in the One True God."

Her voice wavered like a candle in the wind. "So that's how to be born-again?"

The man took his wife's hand. "Shannon and I gave our lives to the King of Kings and Lord of Lords, and we experienced a new birth. There's no mistaking when it happens. Everyone who looks to Jesus and trusts their lives to him will get eternal life in return, the real thing. God didn't go to all the trouble of sending his One and Only Son to condemn people. He loves us all with a never-ending love."

"I do think it's possible that Jesus is God, and a bigger God at that." Her voice was weak.

"Jesus is one with the Father. It's hard to understand, but it's true."

"I believe in the Savior."

"Good, now don't be afraid to go deeper, way deeper. Find out who that Savior really is, Jennalee, and when you do, you will know Him."

She looked at the time on her cell phone. "I've really got to go, but thanks for talking to me about all this, especially about being born-again."

At the door, Pastor Ron said, "Remember, God loves even undercover Bible believers."

She nodded, sensing their deep understanding of her. "That would be me. Sorry to be so sneaky, but I can't let anyone see me here."

The pastor nodded. "Our secret, Jennalee. Come over any time. I'm at my church office until five o'clock every day, but you can come here to the house and talk to Shannon, too."

"I can't believe how much better I feel. It's like a heavy wet blanket has been lifted off of me."

"Let's pray before you go, honey," said Shannon. "Did you know I used to be LDS, too?"

They held hands, and Shannon prayed aloud that confusion would leave her and that Jennalee's heart would be opened wide so she could see the light of the true God and his Son Jesus. She prayed God's protection over her, against the enemy of her soul, and for her to experience God's Spirit in a new way. Jennalee couldn't remember ever being prayed for by a woman and was empowered to keep pursuing this new life.

■　■　■

"So I went to see Pastor Ron," Jennalee said, looking up at Alex from her side-parted, long, blond hair. After school they were at Alex's house.

Questions poured out of her now. She told him about the teaching of the Pre-Existence—that people live in heaven as spirit children before being born on earth.

He felt himself frowning. "Now let me get this right. The LDS Church believes people are born in heaven, already created before they are born on earth?" He'd heard a little about this doctrine, but was surprised that Jennalee wanted to discuss it.

"Right, spirit children in heaven have spirit bodies. They need an earthly body to experience faith and joy, pain and sorrow, so they choose a family to join. They know everything about this family, but they forget when they come down here."

"Hmm," he said, "reverse reincarnation."

"Whatever, but I basically think each and every child is in the right family."

"I don't know, but I do know God creates and loves each child no matter who they're born to. Does the Church explain why a spirit child would choose to be born in Bangladesh rather than America? Or die before they even breathe air?"

"I was taught it had to do with how much sin was involved in the Pre-Existent life for that person."

"Well, I can see how Joseph Smith came up with it, using one sentence

128

from the Bible, but I don't think it jives with the whole Bible at all."

Jennalee shrugged. "Beliefs can't be proven either way, can they?"

"Studying and using the Bible in context helps, not picking out one verse and basing a major tenet of religion on it. Speaking of which, I'm reading a biography about Joseph Smith."

She hesitated. "You should see the movie at the temple about him. It's so good."

"This book's called *No Man Knows My History* by Fawn Brodie."

"I heard my father talking about that book. It's dangerous. We've been taught not to question the Prophet's past; we know he wasn't perfect, he was human, after all. And our Prophet Thomas Monson says to 'doubt your doubts'."

"Jenn, sometimes doubting isn't all bad, not if it's a step in finding truth. Jesus' disciple, also named Thomas, doubted, and Jesus showed him the truth so he could believe. Me, I like to study things out in the Bible. It's all there if you look for it."

She sighed in a long breath. "I feel so guilty when I doubt."

"Jennalee, God loves you even when you doubt. Religions can be wrong about what God really wants from us." Alex was distracted by her innocent beauty, the way the winter sunlight highlighted her hair.

"You mean the leaders aren't hearing from God?"

"Huh? Leaders don't always hear from God, that's for sure. Religion is man trying to fix sin all by himself, like Adam and Eve sewing fig leaves to cover their nakedness after they sinned in the Garden. I think Jesus came to turn the religion of his day upside down."

"They didn't like him, did they? I mean the really religious ones."

"No, and I think it was religion that killed him. People want to do things their way, not God's. Any religion can mix truth with lies until you're so muddled you miss the truth altogether."

"Maybe that's why I feel mixed up sometimes."

"I'm only telling you what I've heard from good pastors I've had. Stuff they showed me in the Bible."

"How do you study the Bible?" asked Jennalee. "Show me how."

"Okay, we'll learn together. It's not like studying science, because it's spiritual. Bible study goes better with a lot of prayer. Not that prayer won't help AP Chem, too."

Alex knew he was hardly a Bible scholar but he tried his best. With all their senior homework, they started small, with Jesus' words, discussing them and finding references in an online concordance. He showed her his favorite Bible App.

In the months that followed, some questions were answered, and some weren't, but he could tell Jennalee was gaining freedom and peace.

And he loved her more than ever.

Chapter Nineteen

The Prom of Bitter and Sweet

Jennalee put the finishing touches on her hair and sprayed it, closing her eyes and holding her breath. Prom would be the best time ever with Alex. Their roller-coaster relationship had completely leveled out, and she was sure the dirty snows of winter were gone forever now. Spring brought newness to the earth and to her heart. Her phone buzzed. A backlit name popped up: Nicole.

"Hey, girlfriend," she answered, "wish you were getting ready with me. You never told me who you're going with tonight."

"I've been so busy," Nicole said. "Sorry I haven't talked to you in a long time. I'm dating a new guy, and you'll see him at prom. I assume you're with Alex tonight."

"You assume right," Jennalee said curtly.

"I have another call coming in. Got to go." Nicole hung up.

Interesting, she thought, Nicole hardly dated during high school and now she's with some new guy. Jennalee hoped her friend had finally found Mr. Right. Jennalee smiled into the mirror from pure joy, realizing how Alex was her own Mr. Right in every way. Tonight she didn't want to think about religious differences. Her former dream of a temple wedding was dissipating as she learned more about the Bible.

She was the one who asked him to prom, like she did the Valentine's Day dance. This time, she and Gabe conspired to stuff his truck cab with balloons and hang crepe paper outside it one Saturday morning before Alex was awake.

With markers, she decorated each balloon and wrote some form of *Me? You? Prom?* As she attached balloons to the antenna, Alex came out in his sweats and caught her, giving her an early morning coffee-flavored kiss as his answer.

Tonight was glamour night, so she slid on the special shiny eye makeup she kept in a lower bathroom drawer. An open fashion magazine in front of her, she looked at the photo of the model's eye makeup and, after a few mistakes, applied it exactly like the picture. In the mirror, she tried to look into her soul. Did she look like a traitor? Her parent's conversation from the night before rang in her ears.

It was a private conversation, and the only reason she stopped at their door was because she heard her name spoken. That's why she lingered, straining to hear more through the slightly open door.

Dad's voice was soft, but not quiet. "This is what comes of associating with non-Mormons. Marjorie, I'd rather Jennalee was in wanton living, with wild partying and even alcohol! Rather that, than she becomes one of these so-called born-again Christians," he said. "If she does, she's apostate."

"You don't mean it, Rul," her mother said, pleading. "You know this Alex might convert to our Church if we give him more time. We should talk to him directly and see if he'll agree to get baptized."

"Things aren't going our way," her father stormed. "Rather, our daughter is falling for *his* religion. We're losing her. At least if she was into wild living, she would taste the bitter and come back to the sweet. Now she's confused, full of doubts, and hasn't given a testimony at Sacrament meeting for weeks."

"Rul, you don't mean being an addict is better than joining those Protestants?"

"Think, Marj. If she joins them, she rejects all we believe and becomes lost to us. I deal with these traitors in my office. She can't be our daughter if she goes over to their side, and she won't be in our forever family." He sounded desperately sad.

"She won't do that. I know her."

"Drew Townsend tells me his son Bridger's going out with another girl. Jennalee messed up a good thing for this born-again what's-his-face."

"Rul, you know his name is Alex. Once she's at BYU, she'll find another guy, not as perfect as Bridger, but our Jennalee Eliza will never have a problem attracting worthy men. I have a plan. She wants to follow Alex to Weber State, but I think . . ." Their voices muffled, and Jennalee knew they'd moved further away, to the attached sitting room or balcony.

Sneaking back to her own room, she lightly shut the door. Her prom dress hung near the full-length mirror where she'd tried it on. She'd heard enough to know they conspired to get her away from Alex. They could never understand. Why would her father rather she be a drunk than have her accept Alex's way of faith in Jesus?

She hadn't told her mother of any future plans with Alex, so how'd Mom know she wanted to follow him to Weber State? One of her friends must've told, and she thought she knew which one.

Her mother helped her choose the mint green dress at the mall. It was modest, with a one-shouldered bodice covered in mint green lace. The satin skirt with a layer of mint chiffon formed a perfect circle above her knees. A soft bow cinched the waist. Her blue eyes reflected soft green in the mirror as she put on the white gold and diamond earrings that her parents had given her on her sixteenth birthday. She'd stacked her hair with soft curls set on her head like a crown.

The fresh mint green prom dress gave her hope. Somehow, some way, she would guard her time tonight with Alex, the first guy she'd ever really cared about. Even though her parents were against her future with Alex in it, she would at least have this time tonight. She knew all along they didn't accept Alex, but the reality of it now tore a sob from her throat. She'd never set out to hurt them like this.

Stifled by the warm room, she opened the window and took a deep breath of the cool April air. In spite of everything, she resolved that, for the night of senior prom, she would be 100 percent with Alex. Nobody could take this happy memory away from her.

■　■　■

"Smile, Jennalee," said her mother sweetly, "you'll have these pictures forever, and you want to look good! Stand closer to her, Alex. There, perfect." She clicked her phone camera. Jennalee's dad was out on Stake business but came inside just as she and Alex were getting ready to leave.

His eyes stone cold, he shook hands with Alex. Jennalee found she couldn't look at him. Her four little brothers ran up the stairs from the basement family room to stare at the couple, laughing as they went back down.

"Sorry to be late," Dad said. "A serious case came up. Apostasy."

Jennalee knew the comment was directed towards her, a reminder that if a person denied the Mormon Church was true after testifying in public that it was, it was equivalent to blaspheming the Holy Spirit in the LDS Church. It was the unforgivable sin, apostasy. Her father, as Stake president, presided over the meetings that decided the punishments of such people. She used to have nightmares of ending up in one of these meetings.

"Take care of my daughter," Dad said. "And bring her back by 11:30, or she might turn into a pumpkin." He gave her a loving wink, and Jennalee felt familiar pink spots bloom like twilight stars on her neck. Her dad did love her.

"I'll have her back, Mr. Young," said Alex, looking directly into her dad's face, which was more than she could do, though she was as good at hiding her emotions as her father.

"The wrist corsage is beautiful," her mom said, gushing. "Here, honey, show it off in this next picture. Flowers fade fast, and we need one more picture of you both with Jennalee's father."

Smiles faded as fast as the fresh flowers, and Jennalee wondered what she would think when she saw these pictures later. What did their future hold? At least the pictures preserved the moment, her in the mint dress and Alex in his tux, topped with his lopsided smile. And she'd remember how when he first saw her standing on the Young's wrap-around porch, Alex had said one word: "Wow."

They drove over to his tiny house. "Your parents are nice people, Jenn," Alex said.

"Uh huh," she murmured. She hoped they'd always be nice to him. She loved them and she was beginning to love Alex, too.

Alex's mom waited for them, sitting on the cement box of a porch in her jeans. Gina raved over the chiffon dress and Jennalee's pretty hairdo. Gabe stood back, smiling sheepishly like her little brothers had.

"Sorry, Mom, time to go," Alex said. "We've got reservations at La Caille."

"Oh, Alex," said Gina, "what a great place to take Jennalee. You'll both love it!" She hugged each of them. As always, Alex gave her a lingering hug back. "Enjoy your evening. You only go to one senior prom in your life. If you have any leftovers from La Caille, think of us, right, Gabe?"

Jennalee was free from her troubles while riding in Alex's truck. He'd kept one of the balloons with her writing on it, near the mat where she'd kicked off her silvery heels. They drove until just off Wasatch Boulevard at the entrance of Little Cottonwood Canyon, where Alex steered his truck on to a red-bricked road, ending at a fairytale country chateau with flowers, flags, pinnacles, and vine-covered mullioned windows. It was a dream come true for a romantic date.

"Whoa, Alex. I've heard of this place, but I've never been here, and to think our first date was at McDonald's. We've come a long way." She giggled.

"Stick with me, babe. Best French restaurant in Salt Lake. Not that I've ever been here either, but a guy from our church is a pastry chef here. It's fancy, all right, like he said."

The *maître d'* seated them at a private candlelit table for two covered in silk brocade and white linen. It overlooked a courtyard filled with trees wrapped with tiny white lights and mirrors of softly lit pools of water. Peacocks walked the grounds. She wondered if it looked like Provence. Even if it didn't, she'd pretend it was the south of France.

"Robert Redford probably comes here when he's in the city away from his Sundance retreat," she said in admiration. "Bet it reminds him of Europe."

"Let's ask the waiter about him." Alex wished the man a good evening and asked.

"But of course, Monsieur Redford comes here. I see him myself, many times." Then he stood by, waiting for their order.

She read items on the menu with a pronounced accent, making Alex laugh. "You order for me," she prompted. "I don't know what to choose."

135

"We'll start with crab cakes, then."

"Perfect; I don't like *escargot*. Not that I've ever tried snails."

The sun set in a golden gleam through the trees and after they ate spinach salad, the *entrées* came with Alex's fish with *aioli*, and her own plate, artistically inspired *coq au vin*. It melted in her mouth with flavors she'd never tasted before.

"The flavor has a bite to it."

He looked amused, his face lit by candles. "It's the *vin* in your *coq au vin*."

"You mean wine? Oh-oh." She felt a hot flush over her face.

"It's okay, the alcohol completely evaporates in the cooking process."

She was relieved. At least it wasn't like drinking wine. The waiter asked if they wanted dessert.

"Thank you, no, I'm full," she said.

"But we have to try the *crème brulee*," Alex told the waiter, holding up one finger. "*Avec* two forks, *s'il vous plait*."

"This place is terribly expensive, Alex." Gratitude overcame her, knowing how hard he worked all through senior year. "You're probably spending your whole paycheck."

"Try two paychecks, but you're worth it, Jennalee." Discouraged after what she heard her mom and dad say about her, it was good to be "worth it." The waiter returned, and they swirled their forks in the caramel-covered dessert.

"I think about my dad during April," said Alex. "He died on April 5th."

"That's tomorrow. How sad, Alex. Tell me more about him."

Alex's face gleamed with memories. "He was funny, but sometime he could be serious as heck. He was an Air Force pilot. He met my mom at Aviano Air Base in Italy, where she worked as some kind of secretary. Anyway, they eloped when he got sudden orders to come back to the States. They ended up at Hill Air Base when they were first married. I think that's why she wanted us to move here."

For the first time, she saw Alex's strong exterior crumble. His eyes filled with tears. She didn't know what to say, so she took his hand across the table.

"He looked so different, Jenn, as he lay dying. He was a strong man, six-foot-three; he was just the best guy ever. He wasn't perfect, but you could count on him to love you no matter what. Anyway, the cancer made him into skin and bones, frail like an old man, and he was only 45. His hair came out in clumps from the chemo. I wish he hadn't tried to fight it with chemo. It only gave him an extra month and made him worse." He shook his head and a tear rolled on to his white collar where it gleamed in the candlelight before it melted into the fabric.

Wiping his cheek and sniffing, he continued, "Sorry, the worst thing was that none of us could do anything about it. He knew early on and fought a brave fight. He prayed for us from his bed at hospice and said he wished he didn't have to leave us."

"What did he pray?"

"He asked God to take care of us," said Alex, "and to bless us with long and happy lives. Then he went into a coma that lasted for a day and a night. My mom was holding his hand when he passed into heaven, but my brother and I were asleep."

Jennalee tasted the sharpness of his pain, and she didn't know what to say. But in that moment, she felt closer to him than ever before. The waiter slipped the bill in on a tray, and Alex put carefully counted fresh bills on it. "Tell Chef Kevin this is awesome *crème brulee*." The waiter said he would.

"One sec," Alex said and went to the men's room, coming back with a freshly washed face. He'd tamed his hair tonight in a *GQ* way, looking as good as a cover model, she thought.

"Let's walk around outside in the courtyard and then go to the dance. We have plenty of time," she told him. Alex helped her put on her white bolero jacket, and they strolled around in the romantic gardens. Resting on a bench near the arched bridge, he held her hand tight, like he was possessive of her.

"I'm sorry," he said, "I shouldn't talk about all that. I hope I didn't ruin your dinner."

"It's okay. I'm grateful you told me, Alex. I only wish I could help with your grief." She squeezed his hand.

"That means a lot to me. What I really want to tell you is it changed my life forever, and I don't look at anything the same way. It's why we have to grab every day and do all we can to make the world better. I want to be a doctor, so I can help people, stop them from dying. I want to be the best diagnostic doctor ever. There were so many mistakes with my dad's case."

"You'll achieve it, too, Alex, I know you will. You and poor Gabe have had to go through what most people experience later, when they're older."

"Some people are angry at God when their parents die. But the night Dad died, I had a dream that I've only told my mom and Gabe. Now I can tell you."

"Go on." How real he was. No posturing, no posing. How strong in the face of hopeless odds.

"In my dream, Dad came and sat on the edge of my bed, and his face was lit up by a shaft of light shining on him from above. He looked really young, like in his wedding picture before I was born, and he was completely relaxed, no more pain."

"Did he talk to you?"

"Not in words, but in my mind, he related to me not to worry about him anymore, not to be sad. He said he was in a happy place and he wanted me to be happy, too."

"Was your dream at the same time he died?"

"It must've been. The night he died I'd fallen asleep, and I've always thought he came to me right then to comfort me. I'll never forget that dream, Jenn. So, see, I'm not mad at God. Cancer, yes, but not God. That's why I can't change my faith. My dad led me to the Lord and I'd be a terrible son if I changed. I want to see him again, to follow in his footsteps. If I joined another religion, how would I be able to follow him?"

Jennalee's heart fluttered. With her recent personal doubts, here was a young man professing his father's faith and wanting to follow his dad to heaven. Pastor Ron had asked her what Alex had at stake if he left his faith for hers. Now she knew why it would be injurious for him to convert to her religion. She wished she could find the close relationship with Jesus he had. How could she think that any other young man she knew could ever stand next to Alex Campanaro in strength of character?

"You're a lot like your father, Alex."

"Why?"

"Sometimes you're funny, but other times you can be serious as heck."

Alex laughed, a good strong laugh, and hugged her with the same long, lingering hug he gave his mother. It was a warm and meaningful embrace, almost better than a kiss. Then they climbed into his truck to drive to the senior prom. Jennalee watched the lights of La Caille Restaurant fade in the rearview mirror, knowing she and Alex were on a new road, one they'd travel together. She whispered a prayer for courage.

■　■　■

When they arrived at the Utah State Capitol Building where Davis High's senior prom was held, Alex's cell phone already flashed eight-thirty. She noticed most of the girls had removed their uncomfortable shoes and danced barefoot, but the hard marble floor was cold, so she kept hers on.

"We better hit it," he said. "The whole thing's over at ten." He took Jennalee's hand and walked her out to the dance floor.

"Hey, you two," said a familiar voice, "why are you so late?" Jennalee and Alex stopped dancing and saw Tony Morris, minus his kilt, wearing a tuxedo and neon pink cummerbund. On his arm a girl dressed in electric blue said, "Hi."

For a moment, Jennalee couldn't place her. "Oh . . . Corinne!" she said finally. "You got contacts? What great hair." The shy, smart girl looked truly pretty.

"Wait a minute, Scottie," said Alex to Tony, "you don't go to our high school. How'd you two meet up?"

Tony winked at his date. "I get around. It was at the Battle of the Bands, wasn't it, Corinne? I bet you didn't know she plays trombone, too."

"Well," said Jennalee, mustering poise, "you two make a good-looking couple."

Alex agreed with a nod.

"Senior prom has its surprises," he said to her later on the dance floor. "Another mixed religion couple."

"Tonight, we're not talking about religion," she responded, "but look at them! They're both great dancers." The song ended, and Tony went over to talk to the DJ. Alex and Jennalee helped themselves to punch, when over the sound system came a lovely slow song.

"They're playing our song, Jenn," said Alex. "May I have this dance?" He took her smoothly back to the dance floor. His smoky two-day stubble and tanned face contrasted against the white collar of the tuxedo. She thought him the handsomest man in the room.

"Our song? I didn't know we had one. What's it called?"

"It's 'I Will Be Here' by Steven Curtis Chapman. Listen to the words. It's our song all right," he whispered into her ear.

They slow-danced, close together, her head on his chest. She felt his strong hand on her back and listened to the lyrics. Words of serious loyalty and forever love, saying that no matter what happened, they would stick together. She wished with all her heart Alex really *would* be with her always.

Some couples stepped off the floor at the sound of an unfamiliar Christian love song and stood watching Alex and Jennalee in the middle. The music floated through the marble halls, and Jennalee knew there'd be no looking back, that Alex was for her, and she was for Alex.

"You were right; it's our song," she said. "It's the most beautiful song I've ever heard." The music ended, and she saw Tony run across the floor to get his iPod back from the DJ. She'd have to remember to tell him how grateful she was for that gift of music to her and Alex.

She looked up at the Capitol rotunda's columns. Artificial light glared over the atrium where they danced, not like the soft light of the French restaurant. And stark reality jolted her back to the present.

"Do you realize we graduate in less than a month?" she asked.

"Right," Alex said. "And I turn 19 next Thursday."

She swallowed. "So your dad died right around your birthday."

"Four days before I turned 16, and it was so hard to keep up in school that Mom let me take a break, so I'm six months behind. But it's all good, Jenn. Remember my dream? Dad told me to be happy, and I am because I'm here with you. Let's go check out the cake." He was smiling, his grief wiped away for the moment.

Standing in front of the refreshment table, Jennalee could see Cory Talmadge glaring at her from behind the punch bowl. He was with Talia, one of the most mischievous girls from their ward. What were those two up to?

Madeline Silva helped herself to the punch. She wore a coral satin dress with dyed-to- match shoes. Was it her imagination, or was Madeline looking at her, too? No, she was watching her date across the room, Roy Newman from Layton. It was then that she spotted Nicole in a black dress dancing with a tall guy. A glimpse of red hair told her who it was. Her heart lurched. Bridger Townsend was too old to be at a high school prom, yet here he was.

Alex saw him, too. Showing no emotion, he said, "What do you know? He's at our senior prom. Isn't he too old for this?"

"I'm never talking to Nicole again," Jennalee said, imagining smoke coming from her nostrils.

"Why not? Did she take your old boyfriend?" Alex said, so calmly it hurt her ears.

"No, Alex, I could care less about him. But she called me today and didn't tell me he was her date. She did it on purpose to upset me."

"We can leave if you want to, Jenn."

"Can we? Let me make a pit stop at the ladies' room first."

"I'll get your jacket and meet you on the stairs. Hey, thanks for the slow dance."

■　　■　　■

Later, he knew if he hadn't stopped to talk to Tony so long, it never would've happened. Misjudging the time that Jennalee would be out and ready to meet him on the stairs was his mistake. He searched the dance floor and hallways in the glaring light, then went back to the stairs to see if she was there, and he'd only missed her. But she was nowhere to be seen.

His Italian-made shoes with their soft leather soles were noiseless on the marble stairs, so no one heard him turn the corner, where he caught muffled sounds coming from the shadows between two columns. A hulk of a guy had his hands all over a squirming girl. The flash of mint green chiffon told him it was Jennalee. His hands formed fists as he approached.

He could see her struggle to keep Bridger off, but she wasn't screaming yet. Alex felt adrenaline pump through his veins and a loss of control overtook him. He grabbed the big guy's shoulder with hard fingers in a claw. Bridger moved slightly and only later guessed who hit him.

Jennalee stepped away from the staggering Bridger. Blood spurted from the guy's nose as Alex stood his ground, hands ready for action, expecting the big gorilla to come at him. Instead, Bridger cowered and ran into the men's room holding his nose and howling.

Grabbing Alex's hand, Jennalee said, "Let's get out of here." They ran, her other hand holding the bodice of her dress. Her heels caught in the torn chiffon hem as she stumbled into the truck. Alex opened the door and helped her inside, safe.

■　■　■

"He hurt you, didn't he?" Alex asked once they were inside, parked, with the heater on full blast.

Jennalee glanced at her shoulder. "He tried to claw part of my dress off, but I'm okay. I couldn't find you, Alex. I went downstairs twice thinking you could be there. He was down there, even being nice to me, but he suddenly changed his mood and grabbed me and started groping." She shivered.

Alex stared at the wheel, chin down. "I'm sorry. I stopped to talk to Tony and lost you. That guy's crazy; he's an animal. I ought to go back and punch him out." He smacked the dashboard with his fists.

"It's okay. You came just in time; he didn't do anything too bad." She looked down at the ripped lace on her dress and Alex helped her put on her jacket. "He scared me, though, and I never want to see him again. Can you believe my parents prefer him over you? How could they?" Sobs broke loose from her.

He kept his voice quiet. "You need to tell them about this." He put his arms around her as best he could in the pickup just to make her feel safe.

"They'd never believe me. Brent warned me about Bridger, and he was right." She took a deep breath. "Just so they don't blame you for this ripped-up dress, can we go get some glue or something? Anyway, we'd better get going before the Capitol Security Guards show up."

Chapter Twenty
Persecuted Not Abandoned

Starbucks was crazy busy during his shift, but Alex kept up as best he could, brewing hot combinations of cream and espresso shots.

"How's it going, Alex?" said a middle-aged guy in a leather jacket. It was Jeff Allred, the former Mormon who'd befriended him.

"Jeff! Haven't seen you for a while. As you can see, I've been working a lot."

"That's what your mom said. I stopped by your house and she said you were here. Got a break coming up?"

Alex nodded. "I'll take one right after your order. What can I get you?" They sat in a corner of the café, and Alex related the whole prom story. "We'll see if Bridger dares to come around my girl again."

"Sounds like a fight I got into over my ex-wife, only she liked guys fighting over her. She left me for another man a few years ago. Took the kids with her."

"That's sad," Alex said, "is she still Mormon?"

"Yeah, she didn't want me after I became born-again. I guess I changed too much for her. At least I get to see my kids a lot, they live close by."

Alex pitied Jeff. He'd given up his family to become a Christ-follower. "How old are your kids?"

"Twins, a boy and a girl about your brother's age. Just saw him at your house. He's about fifteen?"

"Gabe's fourteen. Hey, we'd love it if you brought them over to shoot hoops sometime."

"Thanks. Sometimes they get bored in their old dad's apartment. So back to your life. What ended up happening after prom? You're not in jail for assault."

"Nope. Imagine what my mom would've done if that'd happened. Jeff, I was surprised I got so mad, but I couldn't help it. We ran away before anyone noticed, got into the truck, and went home. No teachers came, no guards, so Bridger must've had to explain why his nose was bloodied all by himself, I guess. And I bet he didn't tell the truth."

"Hit and run, huh?" Jeff said, laughing. "You could've been in jail if those Capitol Security Guards would've caught you. 'Course they were on light duty at the prom."

"Yeah. But just to be serious for a sec, I've got a lot against me right now. When they find out, her parents will make this gentile history." He slumped lower in his chair.

"I have a Scripture for that—Romans 8:37. 'We are more than conquerors through him who loved us.' When you have everything against you, remember that. It's one of my favorites, along with end of Chapter 8: 'Neither death nor life, neither angels nor demons, neither the present nor the future, nor any powers, neither height nor depth, nor anything else in all creation, will be able to separate us from the love of God that is in Christ Jesus our Lord.'"

The Word filled his ears, bringing its power with it. "You memorized that?" Alex asked.

"I've got a lot of time on my hands, being a bachelor again. Not much to do in a tiny apartment. You memorize it, too, buddy. You're going to need it."

"Stuff is piling up. On top of everything else, I've been offered a job, a good one. It's a chance to learn my uncle's business for a year, only it's in Italy and starts this summer. I don't want to leave Jennalee, so I may have to say no."

"Whoa, a job like that sounds too good to let go. See what she says. You two need to be open with each other about your futures. I hate to say this, but as young as you are, it may be good to separate for a season. And real love lasts, even when you're apart."

"Separate? I don't know. She said she wanted to take a gap year before college and I just thought she could go to Italy, too."

"From what you've told me, she's LDS through and through. They don't take gap years, they go on missions. Either that or her folks will hustle her on over to BYU faster than you can say 'graduation'."

"Wait a minute, Jeff, she's changed since I talked to you last. The New Testament is speaking to her, and she's learning about Jesus, the real one."

"Okay, Alex, but from my perspective, to unlearn religion and learn how to be a true Christ-follower is a process. It can take time."

"We don't have time. I don't want to lose her because I know she's the one I eventually want to marry. I want the job, but I don't want to be away from her."

"You're a smart guy, Alex, and I know God will help you figure it out."

"Hope so. Another thing is, my mom's dating a new guy and she could move if she marries him. So I've got to think about my brother, too. We don't exactly like the guy that much."

Jeff's look of concern got deeper. "No wonder God gave me the impression I should talk to you today. I'm going to step up my prayer for you. I can see you love that girl, so my best advice is to go talk to Pastor Ron and bring your girl with you."

■ ■ ■

Pastor Ron welcomed them into his office. Alex was anxious to find out how he and his wife weathered dating, marrying, and staying together even though she'd grown up LDS. He and Jennalee faced obstacles before, but now they were blockaded. Alex hadn't told her about the year-long job in Italy yet. He was afraid to.

"Niceties aside, I'll cut to the chase," said Pastor Ron. "First, I'm glad you're here. I'm amazed at such faithfulness to God and each other that you would come and ask for advice and prayer."

Alex cleared his throat. "We're graduating next month and forces beyond our control may split us up. How can we stay together with everything against us?"

Jennalee looked hard at him. "What forces, Alex?"

Pastor Ron said, "I think Alex means religion, parents, college, jobs. Isn't that right?"

Alex nodded.

"I imagine you've already had discussions about your futures."

"We have," answered Alex, "but the main concern is religion. Jennalee's read the Gospel of John and is understanding the difference between our gospel and the LDS one."

Jennalee took his hand. "I do have trouble unlearning what I was brought up to believe. And I'm afraid to face my parent's disapproval in all of this."

"Understandable," said Pastor Ron. "Go on, Jennalee."

"My father might disown me if I wasn't LDS anymore, but I think my mom would try to change his mind. Alex can't become LDS, so we're in a dilemma. Did your wife's family disown her?"

"She lost them for a time, but they're back in our lives. We all realized that we love each other enough to have a good relationship in spite of our differences. Shannon didn't quit suddenly. In fact, she attended the Church for a while even after we were married. She left only when she had a clear confirmation from God. A year ago, she finally removed her name from the rolls of the LDS Church."

Alex noted Jennalee's pale face. "I know it's not easy to change for Jennalee, but whatever happens, we want to stay together."

"I must admit, you two have a dynamic chemistry. You're in love, then?"

Jennalee blushed, and Alex looked directly at her. "Yes," he said.

"Then my most important advice to you is to stay true to the One and Only Jesus Christ. Love him first, and he will give you the desires of your hearts. Jennalee, be totally open to learn more about Alex's faith. Pray for God to show you the truth, and don't be afraid when you find it. After all, the true Pearl of Great Price is Jesus and His Kingdom."

Jennalee nodded.

"And you, Alex, be mindful that Jennalee is a tender shoot of growth, and she can't bear too much weight without breaking. While she's not quite ready to understand, in his time, the Lord will bring her along, you'll see. Pray, and allow Him to work in her life."

Alex nodded, resolving not to push too much too soon.

"Look up every question in the Bible. Find the answers for yourselves, because I'm not the bottom line. I'm not the authority, just an under-shepherd for the true Shepherd."

"Alex has shown me a lot about studying the Bible," Jennalee said.

"Good—studying the Bible will bring you closer. Let's pray before you leave that God will keep you together. I believe he wants to, but even if you're separated, never forget to pray for God's greatest will in the situation."

Chapter Twenty-One
The Best Ice Cream in South America

In April, Brent spent his 21ˢᵗ birthday in the tiny apartment in Buenos Aires with his friend Ammon singing over a pathetic cupcake. He longed for Mother's Day, when he would be able to call his parents. He'd be home a mere three months later when he could finally see them in person. The two years of his Mission had gone by in slow eons of time, sometimes unbearable, and Brent felt he was waiting for his real life to begin after his Mission was over.

"Let's get our email at the internet café today," said Ammon, the morning after the dismal birthday.

Brent patted his shoulder. "I know what you're thinking. You want to go to the ice cream place across the street. And since we didn't get any yesterday, I agree. My treat."

Ammon looked overjoyed.

The two white-shirted young men locked their bikes and strolled into the crowded internet hub, setting their messenger bags next to computers and emailing the mission president first, then their families.

Minutes later, a familiar female voice said, "We meet again! Hey, Rachel, it's our angels of mercy. Can you guys show us how to log on here?"

Brent whirled around on the white plastic chair. He and Ammon stood up, a bit awkwardly. "Hey," he said, "Alison and Rachel, right?"

"Elder Carr and Elder Young, can we call you by your first names?" Rachel asked.

"Sorry, we're not allowed to tell you." Brent sure wished he could.

Ammon offered his computer to Alison, logging off with one finger. "You can have this one. If you have your ticket, it's simple to log on."

"We paid for 15 minutes. You know, seven and a half minutes each." Alison sat down and allowed Ammon to show her. Alison's auburn hair was tucked up in a bun with curly sprigs popping out of it, frizzy in the heat.

"Thanks for letting me use your computer," she said. "It's so crowded here."

"Elder Carr has one-upped me," Brent said, shrugging. "You can have my computer, Rachel. I'm pretty much finished."

"I'll share Alison's since we're both on the same ticket. She'll be done soon, won't you?"

Logging off, Brent left his place and another patron swooped down and grabbed it. He joined Ammon. "We can do our email later, because it's not every day we can talk to Americans." *Especially American women.* The thought embarrassed him a little.

"That can't be true," said Rachel, indicating a guy on a computer, "he looks American." Her hair was swooped into a pretty French braid across her hairline where her sunglasses perched.

"Good guess, but he's Australian; we talked to him earlier." Brent moved closer to her. "So you two are from the same church in Oregon?"

"Right, on a three-month mission. Alison and I were at the post office picking up a bunch of clothes sent to the orphanage from our youth group, so we decided to stop by here and catch up on email. I don't like emailing on my phone without a keyboard, you know? Josh and Janie, you met them, remember? They're back at the orphanage, painting upstairs."

"Oh, right," Ammon said. "Did you say three months?"

"Yep. After that, Josh and Janie are going to Discipleship Training School for YWAM and Rachel and I want to stay in Argentina longer if we can."

"What's Why-Wham?"

"It stands for Youth With a Mission. You train for six months to go to foreign countries to bring the gospel." Rachel took a deep breath. "So you guys are from the Mormon Church?"

Brent answered, "Right, otherwise known as the Church of Jesus Christ of Latter-day Saints. We train for three months and have been in Argentina for over a year and a half. We've been to four districts; this is our last."

"We hope," said Ammon. "We never know. The president tells us that one of us is moving and a month or two later, it happens. So far, we've been together more time than any of the others."

Brent nodded. Just talking to an American caused a wave of nostalgia for his country. He knew these girls were from a Bible church, and that they were well-equipped to rebuff any LDS missionary tactics. Ammon was watching how he would handle himself. But right now, he didn't care about convincing them about his religion; he only wanted to make friends.

"So do you have sponsors?" asked Rachel. "I mean, how do you fund your mission trips?"

Ammon answered in a quiet way, "We pay for ourselves, usually by working. It's a great honor to serve by taking on a Mission."

Brent felt himself reddening. An honor? A Mission was mandatory in his family. And as for money, Grandfather Young's legacy had paid for it all. He was embarrassed that he didn't have to work during high school like Ammon. He got to play basketball.

"All done," Alison said, jumping up from the flimsy chair. "You're next, Rachel."

Ammon's face lit up as Alison stepped over to where they stood talking.

Brent had an idea. "Hey, we're going across the street to get ice cream at the *heladeria*. It's like Italian gelato, best ever. You're welcome to have some on us."

Ammon gave him a sideways glance. Brent knew he was bordering on rule-breaking concerning flirting or dating, but he was buoyed just by being around these young women. Besides, they may be more open to the LDS gospel than Ammon thought. He knew his job was to convince them that the Book of Mormon was true. But did he really want to?

"Sure, let me finish up," Rachel said, typing swiftly. In a few minutes she stood. Her T-shirt said *God So Loved the World* and had a rugged looking cross on a blue-and-white-swirled earth.

He supposed the shirt was like his own nametag, a symbol of who she represented. Looking at his feet, he said, "My birthday was yesterday, and Elder Carr got me a cupcake, but no ice cream to go with it, so we *have* to go." He knew he was talking too fast, but couldn't stop. "You'll love it, it's the best anywhere in South America. At least most people think so."

"Sounds fun. Happy Birthday, Elder Young. So how old are you?" Rachel asked. He told her and learned the girls were both 20.

Dodging swarms of scooters, they crossed the street to the ice cream shop and chained their bikes to a pole. Inside, Brent used his finest *el Castellano* Spanish and was able to choose some of the best sweet pastries, too. He ordered the most popular flavor ice cream for them all, *Dulce de Leche*.

"Everything here is *Dulce de Leche*," said Alison. "Look, there's even caramel inside the pastries. They're so good, aren't they? Thanks for treating us, Elder."

"No problem, glad to do it. Elder Carr and I put *dulce* on our pancakes in the mornings, don't we? They don't have maple syrup here. So are you experiencing any culture shock in Argentina?" Brent was curious about how well the girls were adjusting to the slums, the food, and the traffic.

Ammon tried to get his attention, but Brent avoided his gaze. He knew his questions were too chummy, and that the Missionary Handbook wouldn't approve.

"Culture shock? It's not bad for me," Rachel answered, "because I was raised in three different countries. My parents were Bible translators with Wycliffe. I think it's harder for you, Alison."

"I admit I'm shocked by the poverty," said Alison. "Most of the food's great, but have you seen what they put on top of pizza? Hard-boiled eggs and green olives. But I like Argentina, wacky pizza and all. Luis Palau is from here, and we've heard him speak. I don't know if you've ever heard of him."

"No," said Ammon, "who is he?"

"He's an evangelist who used to work for Billy Graham," said Rachel. "At our church he told a story about growing up in Argentina. He wanted to be a famous soccer player and his dream was that a whole stadium of people would shout 'Pa-lau! Pa-lau!' Now, as an evangelist, he speaks to huge stadiums of people and gives the glory to God."

"Interesting," Brent heard himself say. The mention of Billy Graham sent him into perplexity, which he tried to hide. In his room at BYU, he'd secretly watched a biography of Billy Graham. He was amazed at the charismatic leadership and humility of the man. He tried to understand the evangelist's message and decided it was too simple. Brent couldn't see how any gospel could be that simple. Surely a person had to do lots of good works to even deserve eternal life.

This Luis Palau he'd never heard of, and Brent wished he could google his name to find out more. He saw that Rachel admired him, maybe like he admired Billy Graham. Her innocent oval face shone in the humid room as they cooled off with the ice cream. Dark brown hair emphasized fair skin, along with would-you-believe-it blue eyes. Brent was nervous in front of her, not like himself. Was he in over his head? Her parents were *Bible* translators, for heaven's sake.

"Argentina's really civilized," Alison said, "in comparison to Uganda where we went last year. I expected poverty there so it wasn't a surprise. But in spite of having nothing, the people in Uganda seem happier."

"Remember the singing at every service?" Rachel added. "The kids had such sweet voices." She looked directly at Brent, setting him on edge.

These girls were well-versed missionaries in every sense of the word. He wondered what Ammon was thinking. As LDS, he and Ammon did cold calling, knocking on doors without much success. At rare times, they saw whole families turn to Mormonism. Their job was to convince people to follow the LDS gospel and be baptized in the Church.

"Hope we can help out some more at the orphanage," Brent said. "Here's our number if you ever need us. We share this old flip-phone." He slipped them a piece of yellow paper.

Ammon finally spoke. "Would you be interested in taking a Book of Mormon and reading it? We can discuss it with you next time." He dug out a blue copy from his bag.

Alison smiled. "No thanks, guys. We have our Bibles, and that's all we need. Thanks for your cell number, though. You're good to have around, especially in emergencies." She tipped her head at Rachel, who nodded.

"You don't know how grateful we are that you helped us that day we got ourselves . . . well, *I* got us into a dead end," said Rachel. "I think that whole thing connects us."

"Connects us? How?" Brent asked. What a strange conversation.

"It's a God-ordained connection, considering you possibly saved our lives and definitely saved us from harm. When you're a child of God and He's the Master, everything that happens is directed by God, it's his appointment. Life events aren't random in His Kingdom. Plus, we all love Jesus, don't we?"

Ammon and Brent eyed each other, and Ammon finally managed to say, "We do love Jesus. We'll have to uh . . . think about the rest, won't we, Elder Young?"

Tucking the chairs in, they walked outside with slow steps. Thunder boomed in the darkened sky, and one of Argentina's famed rainstorms dumped torrents of water to earth, drenching them.

In the rain, Ammon stood stock-still on the sidewalk like a pointer dog, staring at the pole where their bikes had been cabled. "They're gone," he said, "even the locks." His white shirt was already soaked.

"This is all we need," Brent said, feeling deflated. "We had so many things to do today." Ammon slowly nodded. It was their preparation day, the one day for email, food shopping, washing clothes and everything else.

Rachel and Alison huddled together against the rain in the doorway of the shop. "I know, why don't you come with us?" Rachel offered. "We'll drive you where you need to go. This, too, is God's appointment. The van's just around the corner."

Brent shrugged at Ammon. These girls were the most unusual girls he'd ever met, American or not.

"First thing we need is a bicycle shop," said Ammon, as he and Brent jumped into the back of the van.

Brent grinned. "We've had two pairs of bikes stolen. We're getting bus passes. No more bikes."

Chapter Twenty-Two
Struck Down, Not Destroyed

A week after prom, rumors faded about what happened with Bridger, or so Jennalee thought. She loved her life, but under the surface, change was coming. Humming *their* song as she made an after-school snack of apples and peanut butter, all she could think of was that prom evening with Alex. Even the assault by Bridger hadn't ruined it completely. She daydreamed until her brothers surrounded her like a swarm of hungry mosquitoes, grabbing paper plates of apples to take to the basement family room.

Her mother entered the kitchen, her face stern. She parked the mobile landline in its receiver and looked at Jennalee with a vacant stare. Happiness dissipated into disagreeable heaviness.

"I just got off the phone with Nicole's mother. I know what happened at prom. Would you like to tell me your version?"

"Not much to tell, Mom. I had a wonderful time up until Bridger decided to attack me. I thought it best not to tell you what he did, to save us all the embarrassment. Alex saved me from a bad situation."

"I knew it would be dangerous to allow you to go to the prom with that Alex Campanaro. Is his name Italian or Spanish?"

"He's Italian, Mom. Alex isn't dangerous, but Bridger is. He came as Nicole's date, but he came after me and —"

"You're infatuated with this Alex, and he's not really suitable, honey. I think you should know the kind of future your dad and I have planned for all our children. You can't be with a boy who has no future. Look at the house he lives in. Do you want to end up married to someone like that?"

"If you mean Alex is poor, it's only because his dad died of cancer two years ago, and they lost everything paying for his medical bills. It happens to a lot of people. Alex is hard-working and smart," she answered. "He wants to be a doctor, Mom. Don't you approve of that?" She sensed the hardness in her voice; she'd never spoken to her mom like this.

Her mother frowned. "He attacked Bridger Townsend at the prom. Nicole's mother told me all about it. He's not our kind, Jennalee, and you're headed for trouble if you insist on this boy."

"I'd like to hear what Nicole saw at prom. She wasn't even there when it happened. She knew bringing Bridger would make trouble for me, and it did."

"Nicole wants the best for you, Jennalee, like we all do."

"Mom, Bridger was all over me." She paused, seeing her mom's look of surprise. "Yes, that's what I said. Alex punched him to get him off of me."

"I don't know what to believe," her mother said, shaking her head and looking out the window. "Here's your father driving into the garage now. You need to meet him in his den to talk about all this. Remember, he's not only your dad, but your Stake president, too."

■   ■   ■

Her heart beating wildly, Jennalee approached her father's office door. She knocked, and her dad answered with a low growl, like a bear in a cave. "Come in, Jennalee, and sit down."

She settled uncomfortably on a cold, overstuffed leather couch. Her dad sat stiff and tall at his huge cherry desk, one elbow on the table, one hand holding his head. His jaw clenched with anger. She was in for a lot of guilt-slinging and more.

An hour later, they came out together, his arm grasping her shoulder as if to direct her where he wanted her to go. Her mother waited in the hall. "I don't think we need to be concerned anymore, Marjorie," Dad told her. "Her faith is sealed. Isn't that right, Jennalee?"

Sniffing, she nodded. What else could she do? Her father had convinced her to talk to the bishop. And more.

Once in her room, she cried into a pillow. How could she ever stop seeing Alex? Jennalee picked up her week-old crispy prom corsage and placed it on her cheek, thinking about the huge misunderstanding that had just occurred with her parents. She knew, deep down, how much they loved her and wanted her to make good choices. But with their perspective, how could they understand that Alex *was* her best choice? They were entrenched in a religion that made them blind to her heart at this moment, wanting her to obey something she couldn't.

She emailed her brother.

Dear Brent, You're the only one who understands me. I'm in the biggest fight with Mom and Dad. I don't want to be with Bridger, and they can't accept it. Don't be shocked, but I'm going with a wonderful guy named Alex and he's not LDS, but perfect for me in every way. I want to go to Weber State next year, because he's going there, but they've forbidden me to see him again. I'm locked in my room until I sign applications and write the essay to BYU. Any suggestions? Love, Jennalee

She woke several times that night, wondering what to do, what to say to Alex. She'd have to explain it all to him somehow. What would Alex think of them, of her, of the Church, after he heard all of this?

■   ■   ■

She texted him the next morning. Even though her father had deleted his number from her phone, she had it memorized.

We have to talk. Lunch at Pad Thai?

They liked the quiet restaurant near the south gate of Hill Air Force Base frequented by American uniformed world travelers who worked at the base. She'd pay the bill, she decided, because of the awful news she had to hit him with. When Alex walked in, his curls blowing in the wind, she almost broke down with the heaviness of her angst. This was the hardest thing she'd ever had to do in her life. It didn't feel real, and it certainly didn't feel right.

"What's up?" Alex's face showed he knew she was different than the day before. He sat across from her in the tiny booth and took her by the hand.

"I have to tell you something, and you're not going to understand, Alex, because you're not me. You don't live in my house. I wanted to have freedom, I really did, but now I can't." The sequined elephants on the walls looked surreal through her tear-filled eyes.

"What are you saying?"

The waitress showed up at this delicate moment, and Alex ordered their favorite coconut curry dish, the entrée they'd always split between them.

Nodding, the waitress left.

"Basically, my parents forbid me to ever see you again. I'm grounded and I have to go to BYU immediately after graduation. No summer break at home. I'm to get a job there and start classes in the fall. I'm still processing all this."

Alex blinked hard. "We're seeing each other right now; so much for them grounding you. How'd you pull it off?"

"I had to sneak out, believe me."

"They know we're getting serious, I guess. I kind of expected this, after prom."

"You did?" She dabbed tears on her face with a soft cloth napkin.

"All our parents are peeved at us, even my mom. She's dating a guy who's opinionated and prejudiced. And right now, my life's like an earthquake. I don't have any stable ground to stand on."

"Oh, no, Alex," said Jennalee, suddenly drawn into his world, "I mean, that's good for your mom, but not for you and Gabe."

"We'll have to adapt to all this change, I guess. It won't be the end of the world if my mom gets remarried and you go to BYU. But your parents can't watch you 24 hours a day there."

"That's where you're wrong. My father pulls a lot of strings, and he'll arrange for a roommate who's really a spy. It will probably be Nicole, who's not even my friend anymore."

Alex let out a low whistle. "You always told me your life was planned, and now I believe you. Don't be sad, we'll think of something."

She drew in a shaky breath. "You don't understand. I *have* to go to BYU, Alex. I release you from any promises we made together in the beginning. Go to Weber State, and maybe we can see each other secretly." How could she tell him that LDS girls found husbands at BYU? How could she say that Bridger was there, finishing his degree, waiting for her?

"There's something I need to say, too, Jenn. I've been putting this off, and I apologize for not telling you before. My Uncle Lucio's offered me a job in Italy starting this summer, for a whole year. I don't want to leave you so I might tell him I can't take it." He put his head in his hands and sighed.

"You have to take it! It's the gap year you've dreamed of."

"You're the one who always wanted to go to Italy, Jenn. I don't want to go without you."

"Looks like we're separated this summer anyway, because of my parents, so you may as well be in Italy. You haven't given up being a doctor, have you?"

"No, I'm just putting it off for a year if I take the job. Medical school costs a bundle, and I can't start out with huge loans. In Italy, I can make a lot of money and save it."

"Alex, I think you should go." Jennalee sniffed. "It's sad about us, though. Depressing, really, with me rotting away at BYU, and you so far away."

"I'm sorry, Jenn. I really don't want to go."

"We won't be able to see each other even if you stay. And you have a chance of a lifetime to learn a business."

"Jenn, I've been thinking in my imagination that you would come with me." Alex looked at the table.

"You don't know how much I want to see Italy. With you." She set her silverware all in a line. "But remember I told you I'd be stuck in Utah the rest of my life? It's happening."

"There's the option of us eloping." His crooked smile appeared.

"I've thought of that, and it's not off the table, but I don't think I could hurt my parents that much even though I'm furious at them. They think I'm just infatuated, but I know it's more than that."

He retook her hand across the table. "Way more. We haven't overcome so much to give up now. If we love each other and we're meant for each other, this is only a *test*," he replied.

The Thai waitress chose the moment to set down a large bowl of steaming rice, curry, and plates, and scurried away.

"What do you mean by a test?" Jennalee thought all her life was a long test to the finish line, Celestial Heaven. She was curious to understand Alex's idea.

"I had to read *War and Peace* by Leo Tolstoy in World Lit class last semester. There's a part that stuck with me. There were two people in love, Natasha Rostov and Prince Andre. They separated for one year to see if their love overcame their differences."

"Did they make it?"

"Well, no, Natasha was really young, and she got sidetracked."

"I wouldn't," said Jennalee. "If we made a pact like that, I think we'd make it, Alex." A glimmer of hope replaced her despair.

"Unless you meet a nice LDS guy in Provo and get married before I can fly back to stop you."

He would never believe how true that could be in Provo, and how close her parents were to forcing her to do just that. Only Bridger was not a nice guy.

Jennalee removed her hand from his, and took some rice, giving the coconut curry to Alex. "It smells wonderful, but my stomach's all weird over this. You go ahead and eat it. I'll just have some rice." Her destiny was *not* going to be a married student at BYU. "You're worried about *me* staying single? What about you? Your family will set you up with some nice Italian girl."

He laughed. "Yeah, they always try to match me with girls, Nonna, especially. If I go, I'm learning the family business, nothing else. Listen, I don't want to be a jealous, possessive guy when we're apart. You don't want me that way, either. I promise I will be true to you. There's only one girl in the world I care about. You, Jenn."

She loved him in that moment. "Oh, Alex, I'll be true to you, too. I just wish I was free. They're clipping my wings. Maybe I can run away."

Alex exhaled. "Wish you could. Graduation's almost here. We both knew this time would come. I don't know what I'm going to do without you."

"I wish I could trade your life with mine," she said.

"I wouldn't make a very good BYU student. They'd make me shave every day and cut all my hair off. And you wouldn't make a very good wine merchant either."

Was he kidding? The very mention of wine was scary to her, foreign and strange. "I don't know the first thing about wine, but I may pull it off, I'm used to being an actress."

"My friend Jeff says there are seasons in your life. If we make it through this season of being apart, and we stay together in love through it all, we have something a lot of people never have." He inclined his head close to hers. "The real thing."

She wanted to cry. He was leaving and she couldn't go with him.

"So you really think I should take the job?" Alex took a bite from the curry.

Her heart hurt when she said, "You should, and do you understand why I have to go to BYU?"

"You're loyal to your parents and I admire that. Let's make a pact, Jennalee. In one year, we'll meet again and decide whether we're ready to get married. What do you think?"

"Well, a lot can happen in a year, but I don't see that we have any other choice." Her mind went off thinking about all the ways she could parry off her parents, Bridger, and Nicole, so she'd be free in a year.

"What do we tell our friends?" she asked.

"That we're giving it a rest. We can't have them suspect anything. But we'll be together again. In a year, your parents won't be able to do much because I mean to make as much money as I can. That will give us some freedom."

If she could only be free *now*, she thought. "Alex, you've got to communicate with me the whole time. It's too much to bear if I never hear from you." He already seemed distant, probably thinking about his job in Italy. She was in danger of facing a long future without him. For her, it would be like walking along the edge of a cliff.

"Email and text to keep up our morale. Natasha and Andre wrote letters. Open a new address on Hotmail. I'll let you know if I get a new number in Italy, but you'd better get me off your Facebook. That's the first place everyone will look. And change your status."

"Do they have 'taking a rest'? Why can't we call or Skype?" Jennalee could only think it was lack of communication that caused Natasha's downfall in *War and Peace*.

"Sure we can, but we can't get caught. We each have to figure things out by ourselves for a while. I think this is a year to make your own decisions, Jennalee—about me, about your faith, about the Bible."

Alex made an effort to smile, but his voice shook when he added, "I'll pray for you every single day. Let's trust God to take care of us and show us what to do this year. If I'm ever your husband, I want a wife who knows what she thinks and why she thinks it. You can do this, Jennalee. It's what I love about you, your fearlessness and love of freedom."

She pictured herself at BYU, a bird trying to fly through glass. Freedom wouldn't be hers this year. "I'll never forget you, Alex, and what you showed me in the Bible about Jesus. I don't know if I'm strong enough to keep my new faith in Jesus going, especially in Provo, but I mean to show you I can make it through this year. I'm no Natasha. It may look like I let you down, Alex, but I won't, I promise."

"That's the spirit, Jenn. Be strong and always hope, okay? Don't despair."

"By the way, was all that talk about a husband and wife some kind of proposal? Because you'll have to do a whole lot better than that next year."

Alex's eyes sparkled. "Wait and see." He grabbed the check before she could.

"I'll pay," she said.

"You can get the next one, when we meet again."

She gazed at his face, his crooked smile, his hair, trying to remember him forever, in case fate separated them, and they never saw each other again.

"Let me test our communications," she said, texting him.

His phone beeped immediately and he read it. *I love you, too*, he answered.

■　　■　　■

Overnight, her home became as stifling as a hothouse. Her parents barely spoke to her, regarding her with uneasy displeasure. Her brothers whispered in corners. No one was open any more. Jennalee asked for strength from God just to make it through each grounded day.

Only an Oscar-winning actress would be able to hide new beliefs. She had to pretend she was full board for "The Y", as everyone called BYU, but secretly keep her plan to meet Alex in a year.

Her parents had hardly given Alex a chance, yet they controlled her. She had no job, no money, and no place to live. Was she ready to leave them behind to forge her own future? If they were wrong about Alex, what else were they wrong about? She loved them, admired them, but knew giant steps to adulthood were before her now. She could only control what she able to, and that wasn't much.

Up in her room, Jennalee applied for a part-time summer job in Provo Mall. If she lived in the dorms, she'd be safe from Bridger and all men because of the strict rules. Jennalee knew to go along with all the right things, keep a low profile, go to class, and avoid Bridger. Doing that, she thought she'd make it back to Alex in a year. After all, Nicole liked Bridger, and she'd encourage them to become a couple.

She opened her window and switched on her laptop. Her email had several messages, but she opened Brent's, the one she'd been waiting for. It shocked her in the first line.

Dear Jennalee, My advice? Go on a Mission. You'll be eligible when you turn 19 in September. Grandpa's money is in the bank for you, like it was for me. I hope to see you before you go, but I think you'd better go ASAP. Get your recommends. You have to do something drastic because Bridger's obsessed with you. Don't go down to BYU with him anywhere near you. I never thought I'd tell you to do this, but our parents don't understand the kind of man Bridger is. Tell Dad you want to go on a Mission and he'll be overjoyed. I honestly can't think of anything else for you to do. Love always, Brent

So the danger was real and she hadn't even told her brother about the attack at prom. Her previous plans scrapped, she tried to find out about going on a Mission. Their parents would be happy indeed about it, and once she was sequestered at the Missionary Training Center, Bridger would be unable to bother her. In eighteen months, when she got back, he'd have found someone else, and she'd be free.

There was a glitch. What about Alex? Meeting him next May would be impossible. Still, wouldn't he agree that it was better to be halfway around the world on a Mission for a few extra months than to be trapped into being Bridger's wife for time and eternity?

Chapter Twenty-Three
Graduation Day

Graduation evening was cool, with wind rolling into the valley from the still snow-covered Wasatch Front. Alex didn't see Jennalee all week and found himself actively looking for her. She didn't answer his texts or emails. Without communication, he was anxious to talk to her if he could only find her.

By his side in the long line of robed graduates, Madeline Silva laughed about something as she looked at her phone. They were positioned in the front of the line, in a gaggle of AP students, ready to pick up their accolades and honors. Everyone in this group was appalled he didn't go to college right away, but into the wine business. Disapproving glances followed him as he walked up to the head of the line.

In the few minutes before getting into the queue for the procession to the platform to receive their diplomas, everyone took selfies with their friends. "Save my place, Alex," said Madeline, "I've got to get a picture of me and my boyfriend over there."

"Sure," he said, as he felt a tap on his shoulder.

It was Jennalee, keeping her head low, almost hiding behind her long hair and mortarboard tassel. "I don't know what to say except don't forget me, Alex. I'm leaving tomorrow for Provo." Her face was reddish. She'd been crying.

"Don't cry, Jenn," he said, sweeping her hair out of the way and bending down to give her a smile. "We need a picture together." He took out his phone and the two of them looked up for an instant as he hit the button. "I'll send it. And I'll remember you and all our times together."

"I guess we set ourselves up for hurt like this when we started dating. It's all so impossible. Alex, I hope . . ."

"Don't look at it like that. One year, remember? It'll go fast, I promise. I'm leaving next week, and I'll text you when I get to Italy. When you set up your new account, email me. You didn't answer my texts all week, Jenn."

Jennalee looked around like a cornered animal in a cage. She reached under her graduation gown's collar, and pulled out a shiny silver cross, his gift cross. He took it in his hand for a moment, then she tucked it back under her graduation robe.

Alex thought her the most beautiful creature alive in that moment. "*Ciao, bella donna.* We'll be back together again, you'll see." He tried to be strong, but his throat tightened. He hated seeing her cry because it made him want to.

"Good-bye, Alex." He watched her walk back to her place in the lineup.

Madeline bounced back just as Jennalee left. "I didn't really think you'd be talking to *her* again, Alex, not after what she's done."

"What do you mean?"

"Rumor has it that right after you decided to take a break from dating, she called some guy who wanted to marry her. Remember that older guy, the one from BYU? I bet they get married. You know, the one who showed up at the prom."

"Yeah, I know who he is."

■　　■　　■

During the ceremony, Alex had to concentrate hard to hear the names being read. Afterwards, there were pictures with Mom and Gabe, and even Carl. Just when he needed strength from God, he didn't seem to have it. Old conversations with Jennalee danced through his brain. He was certain that the LDS Church had grabbed her back.

Avoiding the Young clan during refreshment time was easily done as there were so many people. He was cheered to see his pastor, along with Jeff Allred. Even Tony showed up.

"Someone told me that Jenn's going out with the BYU guy again," Alex said to Tony and Jeff. "We were only taking a break, and we had an understanding to wait for each other."

Tony looked surprised. "How do you know?"

"Rumor has it." Alex slouched as he took a sandwich on his plate. "A girl told me."

Jeff put his arm around him in a manly way. "That's just what it is, a rumor. I don't think she'd do that to you, Alex. Look at her over there. She's in love with you, man."

"Yeah," said Tony. "Don't listen to gossip. Look at her family. They can't stop her from staring at you and it makes them mad. You can see it all over their faces."

Alex felt better. "Her family's forcing her to go to BYU, so we agreed to a year's separation. I just hope we make it."

"Prayer, Alex," said Jeff, "it moves mountains. It already has, in your case, so don't give up. Simply pray."

Alex watched the Youngs leave the graduation party early, taking Jennalee with them. They probably had a huge graduation party at home with extended family. He couldn't help it; he texted her. It came back: *Wrong Number.* Why did he ever think he'd be able to buck the Church's hold on her?

■   ■   ■

"Over here," his mother said, "let's get a picture of the whole family with Carl. After this, there's a party at our house and you're all invited."

Negative thoughts piled into his mind about this boyfriend of his mother's. Carl would not be *his* choice for his mom, but how could he tell her? It was her life. The man already acted possessive, getting way too close to her. While his mother was grieving his dad, she was vulnerable. And Carl showed up and saved her from loneliness, but something wasn't right about him. Would Mom keep her job or move if she married him?

"Since Pastor and Jeff are here, I need a picture with them," he said.

Carl agreed to take the picture. These photos, taken on one of the worst days of his life, were to stay forever in his mind. It was the day Jennalee left him for a year but at least his closest friends were by his side. They knew about his sadness, and held him up strong. All but Carl, who whispered in his mom's ear while looking at him.

The cool wind swirled white petals from a nearby apple tree around them like snow. His mom laughed as Jeff shook them out of his sandy-colored hair and swiped them off her shoulder. Jeff was younger than Carl, handsomer, too. Close to his dad's age. Jeff was a friend, a guy who'd watch your back. And Jeff could be right, anything was possible if you prayed. He'd certainly do that, not only for Jennalee, but for his mother, too.

Chapter Twenty-Four

Natasha and Prince Andre and the Year Apart

With regrets, Alex took a last look at the Wasatch Front as the KLM airlines plane banked southeast. Only a week ago he'd worn a gown and tasseled mortarboard. He knew he was taking a risk with his college future by working for a year, but the money was too good. His large Italian family would welcome him; he'd missed them. What meaning could God have had for his time here in the Salt Lake Valley? He was a gentile, an outsider in Deseret, and now he was free of that stigma.

He handed his laptop to Gabe, in the seat next to him. "Pick a movie for yourself. I've got to listen to my Rosetta Italian."

"Why?"

"Uncle Lucio told me to brush up on Italian because I have to go out to the vineyards to negotiate with clients."

"You know Italian better than me, Alex. I don't see why you have to study it," Gabe said, settling with earphones and clicking on an action movie.

Alex hit the pause button. "There are business phrases I don't know."

His emotions were myriad: excited, confident at times, scared at other times. Feeling almost abandoned by Jennalee, he looked out the window. She was down there somewhere in that crowded valley. In his desert experience, the only bright spot had been Jennalee, and now she was gone, forced away from him by a religion too strong for either of them to fight. He wondered if he'd get her back in a year. Or ever.

During the last month, he'd recognized that she was the love of his life. There was never going to be another girl like her. Now he was leaving, just as she'd discovered the Bible for herself and believed every word, like he did. He knew she must feel abandoned, too. He'd sent flowers the day after graduation. He'd texted and called her home number, where a young boy answered, telling him to never call back. He suspected their communications were cut off and didn't know what to do about it.

■   ■   ■

Most of the summer was past now. Inside the MTC, Jennalee slid off her shoe and rubbed her sore foot. The new kitten heels didn't fit right. It was already September, and she'd had no word from Alex since their graduation day in May. She knew why.

Her graduation gift was a cell phone complete with a new number. When she unwrapped it, she immediately knew it would split her from her old life, from Alex. She called his number, but never reached him. How unfair it all was, but hadn't she known this might happen if she fell in love with a non-Mormon?

Her Spanish immersion class was about to start. She carried her shoes and limped down the hall, slipping them back on before she entered the room. Sitting down in the back, she stared at the white board, deep in thought.

Her email address was now a missionary one, under the Church. When she could, she filled Alex's old email address with long outpourings of her heart. She'd even tried to call his house a week after she'd moved to Provo. The landline had been disconnected.

She was beyond tears, hoping beyond hope that nothing had happened to him. He would never guess she was going on a Mission. She remembered telling him she wasn't interested in doing missionary work for the Church.

In June, her parents and brothers had taken her out to a trendy restaurant for a grand send-off before she entered the Missionary Training Center. Forced to act like she was happy, she could hardly eat her favorite chicken parmesan. As they were leaving, she cornered her brother, Boston, her last link to Alex. "I need to talk to you," she told him.

"What about?" The young teen acted suspicious.

"If you don't tell anybody about this, you can have my autographed Jazz basketball. Our secret?"

"What do you need?" He was all ears.

"A phone number for Alex Campanaro, or an email address. Anything. Can you find his brother Gabe, and ask him for it?"

"Oh, my heck, Jenn, I didn't tell you. They moved or something. I rode my bike past their house. Everything looks different and the cars are covered with tarps in the carport."

Her heart sunk. Alex's family were gone so fast? "So do you have Gabe's number?"

"I never had it. You know we're not friends. Maybe I can get it, though. I think they're renting the house out to a bunch of college girls, because they were outside shooting hoops. Can I still have the basketball?"

"Don't use it outside," she told him, "or the autographs will fade. Not a word to Mom and Dad, and you have to let me know if you hear anything about Alex, no matter what. Okay?"

■　■　■

It was a long flight to Rome, and Alex couldn't sleep. A nagging thought kept him awake. Jennalee may not want to be found; the rumor might be true about her and Bridger. But then he pictured her in her mint green prom dress. She didn't even like Bridger; she'd told Alex that. But had the adults forced some kind of reunion?

Fervently, he hoped she wouldn't do what Natasha did and get distracted by an exciting new man, crushing Prince Andre. He knew a more permanent separation threatened them. A year was a long time. If they could only make it through and have a happy-ever-after. That was the plan and he'd fight to follow it.

Across the center aisle, Carl sat next to his mom. Mom and Gabe were going to spend the summer in Italy and Carl had decided to tag along for a couple weeks, to see Aviano again. His mother looked happy, but Alex was aware of something phony and wondered if this guy only wanted to meet their

Italian family and worm his way into the large estate and thriving vineyard outside of Rome.

He and Gabe thought they'd get used to Carl, but neither of them liked his teasing, or his sense of humor tinged with ever-so-slight cruelty. He wondered what Nonna and Uncle Lucio would think. Carl had ten days off from his computer specialist job, so it would be a relief after he went home.

His mother was at a crossroads in her life with momentous decisions to make. Mom had subleased the Utah house to Japanese Weber State students who needed housing; she disconnected the phone, and put stuff into storage. Grief chased her wherever she went. Maybe Carl was a distraction.

Needing money, Alex sold his cell phone, the latest Apple model, in exchange for a cheaper one on Craigslist. It was the same red color, but his number changed, right at the time Jennalee changed hers. At least he'd transferred her pictures, and the selfie he'd never been able to send.

He needed to find her fast.

■　　■　　■

Fourteen hours later, Alex spotted Fiumicino Airport and the boot of Italy on the live flight tracker map. After landing, they disembarked into the airport terminal, where Carl and Mom walked ahead of them to get checked through Passport Control.

"You have my laptop, right, Gabe?" asked Alex, assessing all their luggage and carry-ons.

Gabe's face turned white, though he already looked like a zombie from lack of sleep. "I think I left it on the airplane!" he said. "Oh, no. . . I'm sorry, Alex, I'll go back."

"Is that all you can say, Gabe? Sorry?" Alex lost it for a minute, but seeing his brother's tired face, mercy kicked in. "Never mind. Everyone makes mistakes. It's my fault, too. I'll go get it. You stay here with Mom and watch the luggage." Alex raced back. Officials wouldn't let him search the plane, forcing him to go to the lost and found. He gave the clerks his contact information, and for days afterward, went to check to see if it had been found, but no, it was gone, stolen with all of his information on it.

■ ■ ■

Exactly one year before, Jennalee had met Alex Campanaro on the stairway at school. Now she was turning 19, on her way to serve an LDS Mission. Over and over in her head, she heard, "*Ciao, bella donna.*" Those last words in Alex's deep cello voice resonated through her brain, and the memory of him, too, in his grad gown with his dark curly locks and tanned face. She'd never seen the last selfie they'd taken.

Hadn't she tried to tell him this might happen? Now they really *were* Natasha and Prince Andre, backwards in time with no contact. Andre and Natasha only had letters.

Letters? Snail mail? It had been worth a try. Early in the summer, she'd gone to the student bookstore for stamps and paper. Surely the U. S. post office would forward mail to him in Italy. Or the renters would. But she still had no word of him.

She took to praying in the long hours at night whenever she was awake. Wondering if Alex was drinking espresso on the other side of the world, she read the words of Jesus over and over. It brought her a little closer to Jesus, and without Alex, she needed the peacefulness it gave her.

Not that the atmosphere on the Lord's University campus didn't play hard for her absolute allegiance to the LDS Church. Once, it would have been the thrill of a lifetime to actually hear the First Presidency and the Quorum of the Twelve Apostles speak in person. But now her emotions fell flat. Busy, intense classes filled her days, as she learned how to sell the LDS religion.

She scratched at the hem of her new temple undergarments where they hit above her knee. Would she ever get used to them? Her cynicism made her feel guilty. The Church did so much good, and she shouldn't doubt any of their doctrines. Deep shame sometimes washed over her.

The Endowment Ceremony where she acquired the new protective underwear was more her mother's goal than hers. How odd the experience was, ritualistic and strange. Afterwards she sat alone with her thoughts in the Celestial Room at the temple, surrounded by lush carpets and chandeliers, realizing nothing about the temple had monumentally changed her soul. Even the lifelong dream of a temple wedding was dampened. She only wanted Alex to come back.

Her mother emailed:

Dear Jennalee, We are so proud of you for choosing a Mission. To have two missionaries in the family is beyond our wildest dreams. What a good example you and Brent are to your younger brothers. You are a blessing to us, too. Be happy in this work for the Lord, Your loving parents.

■   ■   ■

At least she was safe in the Missionary Training Center. Her first week on the outside, Bridger had stalked her incessantly. The day before she was to enter the MTC, he waited for her in the darkness outside her temporary rooming house in Provo and demanded that she talk to him. She fumbled with her key, buzzing to get inside, but he blocked her way until a night proctor came and told him to go away. His face filled with malice, and she knew her revulsion of him showed. Though he hated her, her intuition still told her he wanted to possess her like she was an expensive car he wanted.

When she got inside, Nicole was watching Netflix on her iPad. "Where were you?" she asked. "How come you didn't answer my buzz? I was trying to get in. I'm late because my family took me out to dinner for my sendoff and there was a lot of traffic."

Nicole's reaction was one of amusement instead of understanding. "I ran into Bridger today, and he asked about you. I told him you were going on a Mission. He couldn't believe it."

"Thanks a lot. Some friend you are, Nicole. You must have told him where I was, because he was outside in the dark, trying to intimidate me just now. You take my stuff, spy on me, then you tell a dangerous guy my business. Heck, you even told my parents about me wanting to go to Weber State with Alex."

"Oh, yeah. That was a long time ago. I never did clean that up, did I?" she answered in a snarky tone. "My mom told your mom about your Weber State plans, and excuse me, Bridger Townsend is *not* dangerous. You're crazy. He's an honorable returned missionary with top honors from BYU. He says *you're* the one who's nuts."

"That's really righteous coming from him. I may be crazy, but I'm not staying here with him stalking me."

"He adores you, it's not stalking." Nicole huffed her way down to the hall bathroom that everyone in the house shared. "The least you could do is answer his affections. There was a time you wanted to marry him, but that was before you started hanging out with that gentile."

Jennalee slept in the shower room that night in her bathrobe. Brent was absolutely right. The only way to escape was a Mission. She wouldn't feel safe until she was inside the MTC and then on a plane heading somewhere far away.

Underneath all the paperwork and busyness to become a missionary was the frantic worry about Alex. It followed her morning and night. Each week came and went without hearing from him. At the MTC, she'd be cut off from her personal cell phone and would only have email once a week.

When she was inside the Missionary Training Center, even her parents couldn't visit her. She was safely sequestered from Bridger, but had absolutely no way to find Alex. She found an old friend in the crowded MTC hallway on her first day.

"I can't believe you're here, Corinne. I'm glad I know at least one person."

"Oh," answered the poorest girl in her class, "Dad sold a car to finance me, and my grandma gave me some money."

"I didn't mean that." Jennalee said, embarrassed. "Where are you assigned?"

"The Prophet received revelation for me to go to Costa Rica," Corinne told her.

"He revealed that I was to go to Barcelona, Spain," Jennalee said. At least she'd be in Europe, closer to Alex. "Good thing I took Spanish in high school."

"I remember. Maybe you can help me, since I took French."

"Ever hear from Alex's friend, Tony? You went to prom together," Jennalee asked Corinne after they were assigned as roommates.

"Would you believe Tony went to Alaska to work on a fishing boat for the summer? He's making money for college. Going to prom with him was fun, but he's not LDS, so my parents wouldn't let me go out with him anymore. They said he belongs to the sectarian world."

"So you don't talk or email or anything?"

"No. We only had the one date. Why?"

Jennalee shrugged. Another dead end.

Her parents told her how sad they were to see her go, although there was utter religious relief written all over their faces. They thought she'd never stray from the LDS faith again after serving a Mission. She wasn't so sure.

All was set for her to leave for Spain in a few weeks, passport and papers in order, her wardrobe chosen and bought by her mother. Grabbing her fat paperback copy of *War and Peace,* she slipped it into a lower pocket of her suitcase. Desperately clinging to this literary link to Alex, she had to find out what happened to Natasha and her prince. Missionaries weren't allowed to read anything except LDS Scriptures and the Missionary Handbook, so she hid it as well as she could.

Her brother wrote often of an American girl he'd met named Rachel. Naturally, she'd be LDS, too, because Brent was too dedicated to the furtherance of the Church to stray away. Would he approve of Alex? She wasn't sure but trusted her brother's loyalty and love for her to at least give Alex a chance.

The very day Jennalee would leave for Spain coincided with the same day her brother Brent came home. Now she couldn't see or talk to her closest brother for another eighteen months. Three and a half years seemed like torture.

A couple of weeks before her launch to Spain, the powers-that-be called her to the office where Mission assignments were delivered directly from the living Prophet in Salt Lake City.

"Are you Jennalee Young?" asked the receptionist.

She nodded.

"Go right in," the receptionist said.

The young man behind the desk was not much older than her. He spoke in a monotone. "It has been decided by the Prophet with the mutual agreement and best wishes of the Missions Board that you are to be reassigned, Sister Young," he said, rattling a letterhead paper with stamps and seals on it. "It is a rare occasion that missionaries are reassigned at such a late date, but there has been an unfortunate incident whereby the previous Sister has experienced a health crisis. You'll be sent to the Rome, Italy Mission two weeks from now." The young bureaucrat put the paper down and said in a low tone, "A real honor for you, Sister Young, since we're currently building a temple there."

Stunned, Jennalee stood. In a shaky voice, she asked, "Rome, Italy? Are you sure? I was assigned to Barcelona, Spain."

"Sister Young, there is no mistake," said the clerk. "You are reassigned from Barcelona, Spain to Rome, Italy. It's an honor and a distinction, directly from the Prophet who received this revelation. You will be immersed in Italian language classes, then fly to Rome. The Travel office is currently changing your ticket."

God had answered her prayer; there was no other explanation. She knew he had heard her, and now she'd be able to look for Alex. It was as though she'd broken out of prison.

In no time, she'd be in Rome, Italy. She'd do some extra homework memorizing maps of Rome. She'd find him, and when she did, she'd give him a piece of her mind for not communicating with her.

She met with Corinne in the MTC Cafeteria after her meeting. Their lunch trays full, she sat across from her friend, and talked above the noise.

"Would you believe what just happened, Corinne? The Prophet reassigned me! I won't be in Spanish class anymore."

"What's your new assignment? You only have a couple weeks, don't you?"

"Rome, Italy. Where Alex is! I'm so happy, I could scream."

Corinne got a puzzled look on her face. "Are you sure he's there?"

Now it was Jennalee's turn to be surprised. "Of course. He has a job there."

Corinne shook her head from side to side. "Madeline Silva emailed me. She said she saw Alex a few days ago. He flew back to Utah, and he's been looking for you on the BYU campus."

Chapter Twenty-Five
New Wineskins

From the top of the down escalator at the Salt Lake City Airport, Brent gazed at his family welcoming him home. He waved to his parents and adoring brothers, Logan, Boston, Jordan, and Cade. His heart filled with love for them.

He knew Jennalee wouldn't be there, but the reality hit him hard. He pictured her waiting for an international flight to Italy, in the same airport at the same time. She'd be excited, he knew, anticipating a new life, even if it was under the strict conditions of the LDS Church. She embarked on the journey he'd returned from. How could he have known that even with its woes and troubles, and perhaps because of them, he would return home completely transformed in mind and spirit?

His grandparents, uncles, aunts, and cousins met him, too. He knew he was much leaner, even thin; they could see he was different on the outside. Inside he'd changed even more and he was eager to share it with anyone who would listen. He put a smile on for them, his knuckles white on his bag, his worn suit hanging loosely at elbows and knees.

His mother hugged him as he stepped off the escalator and his small brothers surrounded him.

Dad, true to his nature, stiffly hugged him and shook hands. "Welcome home, Elder Young," he said with what sounded like pride. Brent felt he was a stranger now in that rigid embrace.

An elaborate catered dinner was brought to his parents' home, and he was expected to speak and testify about his Mission. He fought fatigue so much that his parents allowed him to escape the crowd early after dinner. His Mission had ended honorably, but it tested his character in every way. He knew the next few months may prove to be the rockiest of his life, and felt older than his 21 years.

He missed his friend Ammon, who would arrive next week. "I'm meeting him at the airport and driving him home to Price," he told everyone. "His family can't be at the airport to meet him because his dad was in an industrial accident. He's in the hospital."

"I see," said his father, "I'll help with the trip expenses. It's a good deed you're doing, son."

He was glad to make an escape to his room. His sister was safe now, and surely a Mission in Italy would be less challenging than his own in South America. She'd mentioned dating a non-Mormon and although they'd not spoken about it, he sensed his parents had something to do with that breakup.

Brent held off making his heavy announcement until the next evening, when all the relatives were gone and his brothers were watching television. He didn't want to embarrass his parents or worry them that his new beliefs might influence his brothers, so he chose a time to tell them alone. His father didn't like to be crossed when it came to religion. Brent would have to be clear about the new life he wanted to follow.

"Mom, could you come in here? I have something to tell you and Dad." His heart beat wildly. Though he'd dropped hints in his emails, they couldn't know what he had to say. Mom was clearing dishes and came around the corner with a plate of his favorite berry pie.

"Do you want some, Brent? You're so thin."

"I'm way too full from your delicious dinner. Thanks, though." He took the plate from her hands, set it on a side table, and hugged her, holding on a long time. God knew he didn't want to hurt his mother.

He *was* way too full, he thought. Full of memories, flooding his mind and filling his heart. Pictures of Emilio, José, and Maria Alphonso of the Faith in Jesus orphanage rose in his mind; even the unwanted memory of the mission president's spotless cordovan tasseled shoes. Unforgettable to him was Rachel Christenson's lovely face, sunglasses crowning her braided hair. She made him shaky inside. Yet that memory made him brave, too. He needed courage for what he was about to say.

Mom sat on the leather couch, his dad behind his desk. Perceiving Brent's serious mood, his dad bluffed happiness, saying, "Well, Brent? Was it the best two years of your life?"

He knew he was supposed to say yes and give the testimony he'd failed to give the day before. It was what he was brought up to do. His dad was kind enough to give him this cue, though he couldn't take the bait. Later, he would honestly admit it was those two years that changed his life forever, so yes, maybe they were the best, but now he could only say what was in his heart.

Brent said, "In these two years, I learned I no longer believe the Church is true. I don't believe the Book of Mormon. I am a believer in the real Jesus Christ and his Cross. He guides me, loves me, and I've surrendered my life to him. No Church can come between me and Jesus. I hope this doesn't upset you too much and I love you both." Leaving his parents in shock, he went upstairs to his bedroom.

His laptop comforted him with the screen saver of a picture of his family in happy times. He clicked on his email and was glad to see a short note from Jennalee:

Welcome home, Brent! I'm sad I can't see you but excited for my trip. I want to tell you I fell absolutely in love with an evangelical Christian, Alex Campanaro last year. Needless to say, Mom and Dad disapprove. I don't know what you think, but I hope you'll forgive me if this news hurts you in any way. Alex and I are apart now with no communication, but I will find him and make the big decision whether to stay with him or not. Know that I love you, dear brother, and hope your homecoming is blessed. Jennalee

■   ■   ■

End of Book One

The story in *A Gentile in Deseret*
continues in *A Saint in the Eternal City*,
Book Two in the *Believe in Love* Series.

What Readers Say About *A Saint in the Eternal City*:

"What a page turner! This is the second book in the series, following Alex and Jennalee as they try to keep their young love alive despite many factors working against them. If you liked the first book, you will love this one." ~Bethany

"After having read *A Gentile in Deseret*, I was eager to read the second in the series. I was not disappointed. *A Saint in the Eternal City* takes place after the high school graduation of the main characters. Set primarily in Italy, Rosanne's colorful descriptions of the city of Rome, and Italian countryside make the story come alive. More adventure, and suspense make this one a page turner." ~Jill

"Excellent book. Good information, great story line, cliff hanger!! Can't wait for the next one!!" ~Karen

Acknowledgements

Moving to Utah offered an opportunity to observe a culture that's fascinated me for more than thirty years. I owe a debt to all the wonderful people I met while living in Davis County, Utah. Although I've attempted to relay the Mormon experience to the best of my abilities, I had to rely on research and the varied experiences of those who grew up in the LDS faith.

I'd like to thank Ramona Tucker of OakTara Books for her encouragement and for publishing the first edition of this book. I received invaluable help from Jeanie Jenks, Julie Hymas Gill, Barbara Heagy, Janet Langland, and from my husband, Ray Croft. All of you, including Lindy Jacobs and Amanda Curley of Central Oregon Writers Guild, can never be repaid except by offering sincere thanks. During the course of writing this book and the one following it, I was inspired by Lynn Wilder's *Unveiling Grace.* Thank you, brave Wilder family, for sharing your humbly-told true story about God's amazing grace.

About the Author

ROSANNE CROFT is the author of *A Gentile in Deseret*, a Cascade Award Finalist, and Book 2 in the series, *A Saint in the Eternal City*, published in 2016. She co-authored *Once Upon A Christmas*, a bestselling holiday book published in 2015 by Shiloh Run Press, *Always Home for Christmas* and the historical novel *Like A Bird Wanders* (OakTara, 2011, 2008). In addition, she contributed to *What Would Jesus Do Today? A One-Year Devotional,* by Helen Haidle (Multnomah, 1998). Rosanne is a member of Central Oregon Writer's Guild and Oregon Christian Writers. She enjoys sewing, tea with friends, and Bible study. Contact her at rosannecroft.com.

Made in the USA
Columbia, SC
31 May 2021